HOT SUMMER SAVIOR

J.P. Willie

Nightmare Press
Shepherdsville, KY

Edited by Jacob Floyd

Cover design by Christy Aldridge of Grim Poppy Design

For my fellow Soldiers, Sailors, Airmen and Marines; violence solves everything.

- J. P. Willie

OTHER WORKS BY J.P. WILLIE
Blood in the Woods

"We do not have to visit a madhouse to find disordered minds; our planet is the mental institution of the universe."
— Johann Wolfgang von Goethe

"Courage is resistance to fear, mastery of fear, not absence of fear."
— Mark Twain

AUTHOR'S NOTE

1

I've been excited for this story to debut for a long time. I finished writing it in 2018 and made changes to it for years before seeking a publisher. I started shopping the novella around January 2022, almost a year after I retired from the Army, and much like my first novel *Blood in the Woods*, it took a while before it piqued someone's interest. There are so many talented independent writers, storytellers, and publishers in the world today and I believe if some of the great horror authors of our time were to try to break onto the scene with their stories of terror and the supernatural today, we might not have Stephen King, Anne Rice and Clive Barker.

Hot Summer Savior is a story about the supernatural, brotherhood, courage and the evil that lurks within the hearts of all men. It's a unique blend of war, suspense, and redemption. Once you make it through its extreme violence and barbarity, you'll see there's more to it than just useless violence. Under the insanity there is faith, triumph, and love for your fellow man.

2

At the end of my 21-year career in the United States Army, I *was* William Delequa. The burnt out, angry and exhausted soldier you are about to spend time with. Throughout my service, I hadn't been able to establish long lasting relationships with my peers because of previous bad friendship choices and the cutthroat nature of the Army. So many people were snakes.

I ended up cutting myself off from my peers and others. I viewed everyone as an accomplice, not a friend. I lived my life according to Army doctrine and regulations. Anyone I had something in common with normally wasn't in my peer group, and because I was a Senior Leader, it was forbidden to fraternize. I understood why. I saw it destroy platoons and soldier's careers during my second trip to Afghanistan, so I steered away from that beast. I loathed many of my Senior Leaders (not all of them, but the majority of them) and debated them daily in regard to the way the Army was shifting its focus. I'm a very confrontational person. Hate to say it, but I am. I wasn't easy to work with, but I was easy to work for. Does that make sense?

I believe the civilians and Army leaders put in charge, especially during the Obama years, were responsible for the destruction and downfall of the military, and in many ways, I was correct. Look at it now.

I felt that I was the only soldier left who cared about being a warrior anymore. There were many more that felt this way, especially within the Airborne community, but they were less vocal, because they feared for their careers.

The men that raised me in the Army were hardened war veterans and Paratroopers in the 82nd Airborne Division. They taught me all about being a killer and earning your seat at the table. They knew what it meant to be a soldier.

And I loved that about being a Paratrooper. We were taught to run towards the sound of gunfire, not away from it, and kill anything that wasn't dressed like us. Within the Airborne community there is a sacred term called- LGOPS (Little Groups of Paratroopers). You should research it. It'll help you understand why soldiers, especially Paratroopers, think the way they do. It's a mindset I can't break, even as I type this now.

If you were to close your eyes and think of the word "SOLDIER," what vision comes to mind?

Try it.

Close your eyes and think of the word SOLDIER.

I promise you this: whatever you saw isn't what a soldier is anymore. Towards the end of my career, the men with aggressive mentalities were shunned, bad mouthed and stuffed in a corner and told to shut up and color. Change was imminent, and no one could stop it. I was one of those leaders sitting in the corner coloring, squeezing my crayon tightly with rage and wanting to fistfight everyone in the room. The soldiers and Leaders that shaped me as a young man weren't oozing with toxic masculinity and privilege. They were soldiers and violent men paid to kill for a living.

Unfortunately, the Army now spends more time teaching soldiers about race and gender than about war. It's a business that now panders to the weakest members of society.

Hot Summer Savior was my way of voicing my frustrations and aggravations within my old profession, yet still show the good about the military that I will always remember.

The brotherhood. The laughs. The pain. The tears.

3

Few people know this about me, but I'm a conservative and a Christian. I have been my whole life. Now, now, I know what you're thinking, "He's a Christian and writes this unspeakable and disgusting horror?" Yep. I sure do. I am a Christian that writes unspeakable, disgusting horror and always will be.

A lot of people wonder where I come up with this crazy shit, and to many people's surprise, I base my stories off the evil that walks amongst us every day in this world, and my personal experiences with it. The violence I weave throughout my tales are sometimes layered with supernatural elements and the occult, mixed with the typical jump scares and creepiness most horror writers deliver to their fans, but like I said, most of the violence in my tales are rooted more in real life than you'd like to think. I like to throw my readers into pure terror and tension. You can feel it on the pages as they turn, yet, if you turn a few pages more, you'll also find hope in the darkness. That's the Christian in me.

4

I'd like to talk about the character Staff Sergeant Shelton Hines who you'll be spending time with as well. I based him off an old soldier that I had when I was a Platoon Sergeant in Hawaii. He suffered from extreme PTSD and one day asked to speak to me privately. I shut the door and listened to what he had to say. He told me he was seeing his dead Lieutenant that had died while in a firefight in Afghanistan. I asked him where he was seeing this apparition and he said, "I've seen him in the commissary and at the Post Exchange so far, but I feel he's always around." After the conversation ended, I sent the soldier to see mental health professionals.

That moment has stuck with me ever since, and it is the reason why the character Jason Robertson was placed into the story. I felt grateful and blessed not to suffer from such visions or have creepy apparitions stalking me like that soldier did, because I suffer from PTSD as well.

I want to honor all fallen warriors who gave their lives for the people that stood to the left and right of them in combat. I want anyone that reads this novella that has lost a friend or family member in the service to know that it wasn't in vain. I won't lie to you, I thought about every person I knew in the military that lost their life when writing certain scenes in this novella and I cried.

5

Not only did I base characters on people I served with and the issues they dealt with, but several true crimes also influenced the tale.

Remember the website *Rotten.com*? Well back in 2003, I was stationed at Fort Bragg, North Carolina and I somehow stumbled across a police evidence video of a blonde-haired woman, probably in her mid-twenties, tied to a tree naked and blindfolded. A man was next to the tree, and he sat down to retrieve items from a bag. What happened next, I'll never forget. It took a special type of sick and twisted individual to do what he did to her. That video fucked me up.

Now, fast-forward thirteen years to the end of my career. I was stationed at Fort Polk, Louisiana (it was called Camp Polk back in the day) working as an Observer Controller Trainer. I also served as the Tactical Analysis Feedback Facility non-commissioned officer in charge. I handled scenario development and design for the war games conducted at the Joint Readiness Training Center (JRTC). I started my time at Fort Polk inside the TAFF before heading out to the field Task Force. The gentlemen I worked with there are the best people I had ever worked with my entire military career. They were all retired veterans, hailing from different eras: Vietnam,

Desert Storm, Kosovo, Iraq, and Afghanistan. I absolutely love them to this day. We were able to be ourselves without fear of judgment or repercussions. We were free to be the biggest assholes we wanted to be. Our conversations alone would send everyone into sidesplitting laughter. Though inappropriate, raunchy, and extreme, it felt like the "old" Army to me. I finally felt like I was home. I'd like to thank those gentlemen for a phenomenal 3 years, and if you're reading this Jack, Carl, Stan, Ken, and Paul, congratulations! I'm glad you can finally read, you old bastards!

Jokes aside, working with the bad boys of the TAFF was a blast, but during that time, I learned about a terrible crime that was committed in the training area where the war games took place. I couldn't believe it.

In 1988 a woman, Karen Hill, was murdered and the case went cold until a soldier stationed at Fort Polk, Samuel Galbraith, plead guilty to killing her in 1997 because an old roommate tipped off law enforcement based on a conversation he overheard with Galbraith at a reunion. There were two other murders that occurred after 1988 that were similar, but the convicted killer refused to cooperate with authorities to help solve those crimes.

Karen had been abducted while working the overnight shift at a local Circle K outside Fort Polk. It was close to the main gate of the base. Hours later, a hunter discovered her body tied to a tree in a remote training area a few miles away. The young woman was raped, tied to a tree, and shot in the eye. When the boys in the TAFF told me about it, my creative mind started turning. I had another story to tell. What followed next blew me away.

Unbeknownst to me, I sat in daily meetings with her father, a very strong, respectable Christian man, a civilian who worked with the higher ups and ran the Joint Readiness Training Center. Every time I sat in the daily ten o'clock synchronization meetings I saw him, and secretly, my heart ached for him. I have children of my own and could not fathom his loss. I never had the nerve to walk up and tell him I'm sorry. Since the crime had occurred so long ago, I did not want to open any wounds, and boy, I'm glad I didn't, because the year before I learned of all this, the killer had made parole and was to be set free back into society. By the grace of God, he was not released due to the family being unaware of his parole hearing. I have kept an eye on this case since then, and you should too, because if the man that took that innocent woman's life is released, he will do it again. We must stand together and never allow him out, because he's trying.

6

In a nutshell, that is how Hot Summer Savior came to be, and I must warn you, it's a wild ride, not for the faint of heart. But I ask you to have the courage to keep turning the pages. For many of you, this will be the first time you catch a small, realistic glimpse into the world of being a soldier. You'll also see the world through the eyes of the wicked and the damned.

Are you ready?

Take a deep breath, because one day you might find yourself in a situation where you need to be a hero. And if that ever happens you must ask yourself one thing:

What are you prepared to do?

J.P. Willie

HOT SUMMER SAVIOR

J.P. Willie

PREFACE

Back in 1930, President Hoover ordered the Kisatchie forest in Louisiana's protection due to its rare plant and animal habitation. It is Louisiana's only National Forest. This natural landscape area contains acres of public land for camping, hunting, and recreational facilities. Over 100 miles of hiking trails lay within the forest with fishing holes and cycling trails spread throughout the miles and miles of wilderness. It is an outdoorsman's paradise and wet dream. Longleaf Pines and Flatwoods comprise most of the forest and scattered prairies as well. The timberland is so large it covers eight parishes within Louisiana. Grant, Natchitoches (Louisiana's oldest settlement), Winn, Rapides, Claiborne, Webster, Vernon, and Beauregard Parishes share their piece of the forest with numerous Ranger Stations placed within sections of the forest. Not only is it home to the once endangered Louisiana Black Bear, it is also a simulated war zone.

The U.S. Army Joint Reaction Training Command and Camp Polk use 215,000 acres commonly known as "The Box" for Combat Training Exercises. These activities train over twenty thousand troops and units across the military for combat operations each year. The Box is located mostly in Vernon Parish and began in 1940 as the Louisiana Maneuvers Warfare Training Center serving as a basic combat training installation during the Vietnam War when it garnered the name Tigerland.

Nowadays, units entering the Box use Tigerland as a staging area. The airport in Alexandria serves the same purpose. Not much on Camp Polk has changed over the decades, and soldiers stationed at the installation refer to it as Fort Puke for its semi-isolated location, limited shopping centers, boring nightlife and shitty weather that lasts all year round.

The training exercises are called rotations, and the soldiers assigned as Observer Coach Trainers, normally referred to as OC's, are active-duty service members serving as graders to the visiting units taking part in the simulated war training. The position is held between three and five years and is a strenuous duty assignment that is difficult on the mind and body. The OC's, also called Walkers, are present wherever the training unit goes, always right behind them every step of the way, grading and critiquing the soldiers when necessary. They are nothing more than shadows to the training soldiers. A Walker's biggest concern and purpose is to enforce safety, and with the soldiers running on a depleted sleep cycle, Walkers step in when there's a safety violation or chance of one happening. Soldiers want to die on the field of battle, not while attending a training exercise at JRTC. Sometimes mistakes happen; the OCs are there to try and prevent them.

Prologue:
Throw Me Somethin', Mista!

1245 HRS
15 August 2017

1

Deputy Marcus Jackson rolled his patrol car into the gravel parking lot of Stop & Shop found off highway 121 near Pitkin, Louisiana. The old country store wasn't much to look at. To be honest, it came across as a bit of a shithole most people droned on past, but it was the only option to find refreshment for twenty miles in either direction. Bait and tackle signs covered the once white, outer walls, and a rusted freezer rested against the right end of the building where the Deputy parked. The freezer hadn't worked in years, but locals had taken to decorating it with various decals and bumper stickers which added a spackle of charm.

He swung open the door, breaking the barrier between the cool air-conditioned interior and the oppressive humidity of the southern summer air. He scowled at the hazy coat of grime layered over the green and gold colors of the Vernon Sheriff's Department; a consequence of routine calls in rural Louisiana.

With a quick wipe of his forehead, he cleared the beads of perspiration that had immediately begun consolidating. It was noon and the heat was already unbearable.

A silver bell chimed loud and proud as he entered the establishment, where a yellow sign greeted him, declaring the floors freshly mopped, yet somehow still appeared filthy. The scent of fresh coffee caught his attention. The drink station had several ceiling tiles hanging loose overhead, and the fluorescent light flickered. He hated to pass up a fresh pot, but the day's heat demanded an ice-cold Pepsi.

He recognized the song *Catch Me I'm Falling* from the band *Pretty Poison* quietly emanating from a small radio sitting on the checkout counter. Heading for the Little Debbies on the center aisle, he thought of his wife as he hummed along. She was due in November with their first child and lately the guys and gals on the force were giving him shit over his weight gain. Several Officers referred to him in jest as *Sergeant Powell,* the character in *Die Hard,* because of his robust black figure and similarly, thin mustache. He was quite confounded by the resemblance and laughed along.

The proprietor, Ronald Peters, entered from the back storage room, his voice ancient, yet chipper. "Bonjour Deputy, you here for the usual?" He was once a tall man, but his brittle bones had produced a hunch that took him down a few inches.

"You know it, Mr. Peters," Jackson said, setting the prized cakes on the counter and nodding towards the radio, "I haven't heard this song in forever."

"It was pretty popular back in the day," Mr. Peters stated, wiping the sweat from the back of his neck. "Jesus, it's hotter'n a blister bug in a pepper patch today."

"Yes Sir, it is." Jackson nodded.

"Where they got ya patrolling today?" Mr. Peters asked, scanning each item.

"Well, I'm not gonna be doing much patrolling today Mr. Peters. Don't tell anyone, but I'll be parked off the highway running radar for a few hours. Been getting complaints of folks speeding through the intersection down by the Army's training area, so don't you be doing any speeding today, ya hear."

"You know damn well an old man like me can't afford to be put in the slammer. I'm too pretty for jail."

Deputy Jackson laughed.

"And don't be giving no tickets to any soldiers. You know I served in Korea, right?"

"Yes, Sir," Jackson acknowledged, "I heard you were a war hero."

"A war hero, huh?" the old man said. "That's what they told you."

"Yes, Sir." Jackson said kindly.

The old man scratched his head, his mind wandering back to the men he served with in the Korean War. He quickly locked the dangerous memories back up in the recesses of his subconscious.

"You know, only two people have ever died for you." He slid the bagged snacks over the counter. "Jesus Christ died for your sins, and the American soldier died for your freedom."

The Deputy picked up the bag. He had never heard anyone compare the two and it moved him.

"Now the same goes for you as well," Mr. Peters continued, "putting your life on the line for others. Not many people are willing to do that, especially these days. There's a beauty in that, don't you think? That a person is willing and able to give his, or her life for another in hopes of the better good."

For a moment Jackson thought hard. His old partner had transferred down to Lake Charles a few years back and shortly after was shot dead on a routine traffic stop.

"You know, Mr. Peters," Deputy Jackson paused, "You're right. There is a beauty in it."

2

The police cruiser door slammed shut and Jackson fired up the engine. He grinned as the AC hit him full blast and cracked the drink top, guzzling a good quarter of it down. He ripped open an oatmeal cream pie and began devouring it. It tasted like pure sugary heaven. He followed it with another gulp of Pepsi and a soul-shattering belch. He was feeling quite proud of himself when the dispatch radio squawked to life.

"Unit 3002 this is dispatch please respond," an elderly feminine voice commanded.

Deputy Jackson released a long, lazy sigh, as if he'd done something with his day outside of gaining five more pounds.

He brought the hand-mic up to his lips. "Dispatch, this is Unit 3002."

The response was swift.

"Unit 3002," the voice said, "we just received a call from Camp Polk requesting immediate assistance. Multiple homicides reported in the Army training area. Two victims reported as civilians. The Leesville Fire Department and EMS services are already on their way. There are CID and Military Police units on ground securing the scene for now. Two MP teams have established a traffic control point at the entrance of the firebreak. You should see their vehicles when approaching. The Sheriff is also on the way. Do you copy?"

Deputy Jackson felt a sickening sensation come over him. Camp Polk is a massive Army base with their own law enforcement responsible for providing garrison support to over fifty thousand soldiers and families. If the primary federal law enforcement agency of the Army, CID, put agents on ground out in the sticks, something terrible had occurred. What the hell was going on? This was big for all that attention.

"Dispatch," Deputy Jackson's voice shook from adrenaline, "10-4. I'm heading that way."

Lights and siren disturbed the quiet afternoon heat as he sped from the parking lot leaving a trail of dust.

3

A young Military Policeman, no more than nineteen, waved the Deputy off highway 121 and onto the firebreak that led into the woods. Deputy Jackson returned a nod and detoured the cruiser onto an uneven dirt turnpike leading into the Army training area.

After several minutes the route ended in a secluded clearing in the trees. The ambulance had already arrived, and several military tactical vehicles were parked in a scattered fashion. A red pickup truck, either a Nissan Titan or Dodge RAM, sat in the middle of the clearing. Two soldiers moved through the surrounding trees streaming cautionary tape. Soldiers had gathered in small formations, all keeping their distance from the active crime scene. The clearing was well-lit as there was no cloud coverage in the beautiful blue sky, allowing the scorching sun to burn bright and hot.

At the edge of the clearing, another MP stood sentry next to his patrol vehicle. The Military Police Corps motto ASSIST

PROTECT DEFEND scrawled across the door in bright green and yellow, very similar to Deputy Jackson's vehicle.

Deputy Jackson spotted the soldiers rank stationed at the center of his chest and headgear. Three triangular chevrons stacked upon another signifying a Sergeant. To the right of the soldier's rank was the U.S. ARMY nameplate, and to the left was the soldier's last name, JAGER. His left shoulder proudly displayed a Velcro patch embroidered with "MP," and a 9mm Beretta M9 was holstered on his law enforcement belt. His white face red from the heat, he motioned Deputy Jackson to roll his window down.

"Good afternoon, Sir," the young soldier said.

"How's it going Sergeant Jager?"

"I've had better days, brother," the soldier replied, "I just need to log you into my logbook before proceeding to the scene, Sir, if that's okay?"

"No problem."

"Great. I just need your badge number, first and last name, and rank."

Deputy Jackson gave his information to the Sergeant.

"Thank you," Sergeant Jager said, "make sure you park your vehicle next to that group of tactical vehicles up there and check in with Special Agent Northington. She's handling the scene and can provide you with any information you need. She's wearing a black jacket with CID on the back. You're the first officer from the Sheriff's Office to respond out here. Hell, the coroner hasn't even arrived yet," he proclaimed, "but I need to warn you, it's a massacre."

A massacre? Not an accident or a suicide, but a massacre. Deputy Jackson swallowed a lump of nerves. The worst scene he ever responded to in his seven-year career was a vehicle fatality. A few drunken teenagers veered off the road one late October night and struck a tree at breakneck speed. Their bodies flew through the windshield, tearing them to shreds. He called for backup because he couldn't stomach the sight.

"Thanks for the heads up." Deputy Jackson said, trying hard to play it cool.

The heat had snuck into the cruiser and moisture began to form around his thin mustache. He rolled up the window quickly and drove forward to the scene.

4

After parking, Deputy Jackson stepped out of his vehicle and made his way towards the first group of soldiers, scanning for his contact. His heart beat with unease as an older soldier wearing the rank of Colonel came forward to greet him, his face pale and sickly. The group of soldiers he was speaking to appeared no healthier.

"You looking for Special Agent Northington, Deputy?" the Colonel asked.

"Yes, Sir."

"She's right over there with EMS interviewing some of the survivors," the Colonel instructed. "My name is Colonel Hicks. I'm the Commander for Task Force Five here at Camp Polk. We help facilitate the war games out here. One of Task Force One's Infantry Teams sent the initial report up. Sergeant First Class Delequa is up there receiving medical treatment. He's one of the survivors, but I haven't been able to speak with him yet.

To be honest, Deputy, we're not sure what the hell is going on yet."

"Thanks, Colonel," Deputy Jackson grimaced, "once I get up there, I'll provide you with any update on your soldier I can."

"I would appreciate that," Colonel Hicks returned.

"Let me see what we're dealing with."

"I've never seen such slaughter," Colonel Hicks whispered, his eyes misted with a watery glaze, "Not even in Iraq or Afghanistan. It's a tragedy what happened here today," he concluded.

The statement sent chills down Deputy Jackson's spine.

5

"Hey, hurry the fuck up and block that goddamn area off before some dumbass treads through here and fucks up my evidence!" Special Agent Northington hollered.

One of the soldiers responded with a loud "Roger that!"

She was a very slim woman with light brown skin, yet under her eyes the pigment was darker. Her black CID jacket swayed on the wind resembling a cape only Bruce Wayne would don. She stormed away from the EMS vehicle spitting obscenities. Towards the bottom of her khaki pants, wet bloodstains were visible, still very fresh. Deputy Jackson walked slowly towards the clearing, his heart racing. He could hear a man yelling from the ambulance.

"Hurry up and yank them the fuck out for fuck's sake! It isn't open-heart surgery, dipshits. Get it done so I can call my son back!" a loud, angry voice grumbled.

Deputy Jackson moved closer, the smell of death, stale and putrid filled the air.

Agent Northington spied the deputy approaching and quickly moved to intercept him. He was the first of civilian law enforcement to respond, and she owed him a briefing, but the scene was not for the faint of heart.

"Welcome to the aftermath of a madman, Deputy," Agent Northington loudly said.

Deputy Jackson gave her a quick wave, trying to take in the scene as he drew nearer. Trees blocked much of his field of view. He identified the Red Truck as a Nissan Titan. Suddenly, his foot slid on something soft and squishy. He kept his balance the best he could and looked down. On the ground lay a severed penis, pale and white.

Deputy Jackson stumbled back in disgust.

"Somebody get over here!" he shrieked.

Agent Northington saw what the deputy had found, "I think we got it!" she barked. Deputy Jackson stared at the appendage. Flies and ants covered the impressive member, and he felt his stomach begin to reel.

"Are you okay?" Agent Northington asked.

"Yeah, yeah," Deputy Jackson said, shrugging his shoulders back to regain composure, "Is that what I think it is?"

"Yep. It belonged to one of the victims. Pretty sure the suspect threw it over here."

Seconds later, two military policemen appeared next to them.

"Get the logbook, evidence marker and my camera. I left it on the back of the EMS bumper when I was speaking to Sergeant First Class Delequa."

"I think I need a sip of water." Deputy Jackson exclaimed.

"Yeah, sure. There's a case in the backseat of my vehicle. It's the unmarked Ford Explorer parked closest to the Titan."

"Thank you."

"No problem," Northington said.

Her dark eyes couldn't appear more caring, despite her hardness. He nodded and made his way over to the agent's vehicle, noticing other vehicles arriving on the scene. First was the coroner; the other was Camp Polk's two-star General riding shotgun with the Sheriff, Art Duncan. Media wouldn't be far behind.

As Deputy Jackson approached Northington's vehicle, the entire spectacle surrounded by yellow tape came into view. Pure, unadulterated carnage. His eyes widened as his stomach convulsed. Doubling over, a volcanic eruption of vomit spewed from his mouth.

Part One:
THE SALTY SOLDIER

0430 HRS
15 August 2017

1

D

eep within the southwestern Louisiana woodlands, a soldier slumbered in the back of a dusty HUMVEE underneath his military issued lightweight blanket covered with digital brown patterns.

Sergeant First Class William Delequa had survived the Afghanistan war and remained an active-duty service member in the United States Army. He dreamed a blissful dream; one of memories past that brought great joy. Upon waking, those memories would desert him.

Snores emitted into the morning darkness as crickets concluded their nightly ritual and masked raccoons dashed between trees hoarding all they could carry back to their homes. The military vehicle Delequa slept in was filthy, covered in dried mud and thick dust. The tailgate was down, secured by rusted and aged chains that held it firmly in place, and a white spray-painted stencil on the right side of the bumper read:

5TF-122

A number assigned to the vehicle by civilian contractors that worked in the motor pool of the main cantonment of Camp Polk; the sixth largest military instillation in the world.

Air rolled easily throughout the interior of the vehicle, helping to remove heavy odors and unwanted insects. Thick red mud caked the rear tires and covered the brake lights of the tactical vehicle. Two three-foot antennas for radio communication jutted up from the end of the vehicle, one on the right side, one on left, located inches above the rusted chains. Both are damaged and bent in odd directions from run-ins with tree branches.

Out of the blackness, a young Soldier dressed in full battle rattle approached the HUMVEE, tiptoeing silently, arriving at the tailgate.

"Sergeant," Private First-Class Reggie Calhoun whispered, "Sergeant, wake up."

Inside the dusty, smelly interior, a radio charged in a battery port next to the driver's seat. Its flashing orange glow danced with the darkness illuminating Private Calhoun's strong jawline and good-looking black face. The military blanket covering Delequa rose and fell with each breath the sleeping soldier took.

Calhoun stood at the rear of the tactical vehicle. He noticed Sergeant First Class Delequa's combat boots remained on his feet as he slumbered in his nylon and polyester Woobie. Calhoun mused over the military blanket, or Woobie as most referred to it. It was the conclusive product of US government experiments to simulate God's loving embrace. Calhoun looked around nervously, unwilling to wake the sleeping sergeant, but knew he must; his team couldn't roll out without their assigned OC. Delequa twisted and turned in his sleep, attempting to find comfort on the sleeping mat, which provided minimum relief and protection from the metal lining underneath his body. Calhoun took a small step back, procrastinating a bit longer, hating to wake the salty soldier.

Soldiers that came to train at Camp Polk quickly became aware that Sergeant First Class Delequa suffered from two herniated discs obtained years prior while taking the Army physical fitness test. His twitch reflexes weren't what they used to be, but he was still fast enough to startle. Out of all the crazy stunts William Delequa performed over his 18 years serving in the United States Army, from jumping out of perfectly good airplanes to an attempt at Ranger school, it hadn't been any of these adventures that jacked his back to seven levels of hell. It was a simple timed event of sit-ups that did him in, almost to the point he needed medical separation. One day he was in the best shape of his life, the next he wasn't, and from that moment onward, Delequa constantly chased the ghost of his former self.

Sad, but it happens to the best of soldiers.

2

Calhoun leaned further over the tailgate and gave the sleeping Sergeant's foot a good shake. Delequa's eyes opened at once, heart racing with anxiety and adrenaline. His fight-or-flight reaction triggered easily since his second tour in Afghanistan. He sat up quickly, scaring the hell out of Calhoun.

"Shit!" Calhoun squealed, stumbling over his feet and ducking down behind the rear bumper. Delequa's swiftness reminded Calhoun of the WWE Wrestler, The Undertaker, kicking out of a three count. You wouldn't suspect the man had injuries.

"Calhoun! What the fuck are you doing?" a voice asked from the obscurity.

Staff Sergeant Shelton Hines emerged. His short, stocky stature instantly recognized by his subordinate.

"I'm trying to wake him up like you asked, Sergeant."

"Is it our OC? Is it Delequa?"

"I don't..."

Hands grabbed Calhoun by the collar and pulled him over the back of the tailgate eye to eye with Delequa, who is now unpleasant. His thick cheeks red with rage.

"You plan on throwing a Sergeant in front of my name next time you fucking say it, Staff Sergeant Hines?" Delequa asked, rudely.

"Sorry, Sergeant. I meant no disrespect. I was just making sure Calhoun woke up the right person," Hines explained.

"It's fine," Delequa dismissed, concentrating back on Calhoun. "Never, and I mean fucking never, shake me when I'm sleeping. Understand, Private?"

"Yes, Sergeant." Calhoun replied.

"Good, I'd hate to feed you your teeth."

Private Reggie Calhoun, once a loyal gang member of the BLOODS before joining the Army, returned a nervous grin, despite the deep-down urge to punch the Sergeant in his face.

3

Delequa released Calhoun's collar while patting him on the shoulder, leaned back in the vehicle's bed and tossed his digitally camouflaged Woobie aside. He slid out of the vehicle and stood next to Calhoun. Delequa stretched his aching muscles and looked up to the haze of the light blue moon casting its bluish tint down upon the world. He removed the eye boogers with a quick swipe. Groggily, he illuminated the backlight on his G-Shock watch.

"Fuck my life."

"What's wrong, Sergeant?" Calhoun asked.

"I've only gotten two hours of sleep within the last twenty-four hours because your unit thinks they're gonna win the war out here."

"Well, we are gonna win, Sergeant," Hines proudly stated. "Geronimo doesn't stand a chance against us."

"Keep telling yourself that, Staff Sergeant Hines," Delequa said, half-jokingly. "Geronimo never loses, brother."

"Well, we kicked their asses during the offense, right Sergeant?" Calhoun inquired.

"No, Calhoun. You didn't. Your unit sucks balls, high-speed."

"Aww, come on Sergeant, we aren't that bad."

"Yeah... you are," Delequa declared. "Watching you guys fight is like watching a three-legged cat try to bury a turd on an ice pond. It's ugly, comical and destined for failure."

Laughter erupted into the early morning hours. Delequa continued to gather himself as the two soldiers finished chuckling. Hines provided Calhoun with quick instructions, and he scampered into the blackness. Delequa reached high into the air, giving extra attention to his lower back, the area that gave him all the problems. The metal truck bed never got comfortable, no matter how many times he slept on it, and his cramped body ached from the constriction. Hines removed a laminated map from his cargo pocket. Delequa rolled his eyes, knowing what was coming next, the Big Green Weenie.

4

BIG GREEN WEENIE was a term used by the military when bullshit tasks dropped on soldiers at the last second. It happens to all service members, regardless of rank, during their time serving God and country. The Big Green Weenie eventually fucks all and fucks you good. Better than any dick you've ever had.

Delequa belonged to a group of soldiers and leaders assigned as graders for the war games at Camp Polk, and they were often short on manpower. A common occurrence since no one wanted to be stationed at Polk. It was like pulling teeth to get soldiers to accept the assignment, and who could blame them. It was a demanding job with little to no satisfaction.

Due to cadre shortages, Delequa covered down on Staff Sergeant Hines's Cavalry Troop for an extra day until his replacement showed up, and all he wanted was a shower and an ice-cold beer. Rolling Rock, to be exact.

0437 HRS

Hines walked around to the front of the vehicle. Delequa painfully followed, watching him place the map on the hood and spread it open for the world to see. Reaching back, Delequa massaged his lower back muscles and looked at his watch again.

"What's so important that you gotta wake me up at 0430 in the morning, Staff Sergeant Hines?" Delequa demanded. "I just got back from transporting some idiot from Bravo troop that got himself bit by a Brown Recluse. Had to run him to the hospital on main post since none of his OC's were around. I literally just laid down to close my eyes."

"Sergeant, I wasn't tracking any movements until 0800 hours, but I just got a warning order from my Commander."

"Great," Delequa griped, and squeezed his sinuses to relieve the pressure between his eyes. "I wasn't tracking any movements until then either, but apparently, I was wrong. So, what's up?"

"Captain Reynolds wants my team to head out and establish a listening point and observation post five clicks southwest of low water crossing number five in the vicinity of Khushal village. I'd normally stay back, but all my Sergeants are dead, chilling at the personnel holding area outside the box, playing Cards Against Humanity, and practicing new dick tricks, so I'll be steppin' off with Calhoun."

"Nice. I'm glad our morning is starting off shitty."

"I know, right?" Hines ribbed, "Anyway, the Brigade Commander believes enemy forces will send tanks up Bookout

Road to reinforce Khushal, so we need to get eyes on those targets ASAP if that's the way they're planning to come."

"Awesome-sauce." Delequa stated, bitterly. He knew he was in for quite the walk in the forest.

"Is that the way they're coming, Sergeant?"

"You know I can't share that information with you, Staff Sergeant Hines. I might be bitter and angry, but I'm not a cheater."

"If you ain't cheating, you ain't trying. That's what my old football coach used to say."

"Humph."

"I figured you wouldn't say anything, Sergeant, but I hoped you'd save us some leg work this morning by getting this shit cancelled. It's gonna be a nice hump through the grove."

0440 HRS

"Nice try, but you know I can't march up to your company commander and tell him to cancel the mission. Come on, you know better, Staff... Sergeant" Delequa yawned, "I'm here for you, unfortunately." Delequa wiped his tired eyes. "I'm your coach, teacher and mentor, right?"

"I know, I know," Hines ensured. "It's all good, Sergeant, forget I asked."

"Don't sweat it, killer."

Delequa stretched his back, again releasing a sigh of relief. He scanned the darkness of morning taking notice of blue chem lights hanging from low branches over several makeshift fighting positions. They marked the soldiers sleeping area so tactical vehicles wouldn't squash them during the night as they maneuvered. A generator powered up, and lights came on within the mobile kitchen trailer, aka MKT, about one hundred and fifty meters away. Part of the OCT job was to remain invisible in the eyes of the rotational training unit and not interfere. This gave them the most realistic military training in the world.

Hines sensed frustration.

"I'm too old for this shit," Delequa griped.

"You sound like Detective Murtaugh, Sergeant." "Who?"

"Murtaugh, you know, Danny Glover's character in Lethal Weapon." "Damn... I did just sound like Murtaugh, huh?"

"Yeah, ya' did."

"Fuck my life," Delequa let out a deep sigh.

Hines forced a fake laugh and attempted to lighten Delequa's mood, changing the subject.

"How long have you been a Walker out here, Sergeant?"

"About three years."

"Three years," Hines exclaimed. "That's long enough to drive a man mad!"

"To be honest, it wasn't bad the first year, everything was fresh, new, and exciting, you know the drill. But once I hit the second year," Delequa leaned back against the HUMVEE. "I hit a brick wall, man. I really did, and I'm running on fumes. My fucking branch manager says there's no other assignments available right now, so it looks like I'm stuck here in the sweatbox, coaching and correcting leaders on their mistakes until they find another Sergeant First Class to replace me."

"Damn, I see why you've been frustrated this entire rotation, Sergeant."

"Oh, I'm frustrated as fuck all right. Outside of this being a thankless job, the senior leaders and soldiers don't give a fuck about what I got to say."

"That's not true, Sergeant," Hines said.

"Oh, it's true, brother."

"Well, my soldiers appreciate your input," Hines affirmed. "You've helped improve my troops, and you've made me better. I think through things differently before I execute."

"Yeah?" Delequa asked, slightly amused.

"Hell yeah, Sergeant. You're good at what you do."

"Maybe I should hunt the good stuff, huh?"

"Probably, Sergeant."

"Well fuck that, not gonna happen, home-slice," Delequa said nonchalantly. "I get so fucking sick of correcting undisciplined Soldiers nowadays. Fucking millennials, chicks wanting dicks, dudes without dicks, the Army's more confused than Caitlyn Jenner at a sausage lingerie party."

Hines laughed.

"Nowadays Soldiers don't listen to anyone, or anything, besides Miley Cyrus and that cock- eyed rapper who looks like a pile of shit with eyes." Delequa snapped his fingers, "what's his fucking name?"

"Fetty Wap," Hines said, sadly.

"Fetty Wap, that's his fucking name, garbage, hot garbage, man." Delequa ranted, "and it's Hollywood and the celebrities that make my job difficult. Maintaining good order and discipline nowadays is an impossible task, and I'm sick of the shit. This generation and their entitled vaginas are the reason I'm fucking retiring."

"I hear you," Hines agreed, still chuckling at the tirade.

"It's easy, just listen to what the fucking Walkers tell you to do out here and save the high school drama for back home, because I ain't got time for the bullshit. If I tell you to wear your fucking eye protection, wear your fucking eye protection. If I tell you to wear your fucking seatbelt while driving, wear your mother-fucking seatbelt! Nobody comes to JRTC to die!" Delequa preached.

"Damn, I thought I was pissy, but you're about to have a heart attack, Sergeant."

"Ya think?" Delequa asked sarcastically, reaching into his back pocket to retrieve a can of Grizzly snuff, his cheap and affordable pick-me-up.

"You know, it ain't just the millennials and new soldiers coming in, it's the senior leaders, leaders who've been around the block a few times but feel they have to change their leadership style, and smooch these little fucker's assholes," Delequa confessed, stuffing his bottom lip full of tobacco. "And I get it, I understand no leader enjoys being told they're doing something tactically or doctrinally wrong out here in the box. I've bumped heads many a time with leaders out here, but if you're fucked up, you're fucked up. I'm so over the push back I get. I'm burnt the fuck out with everything, man. I only got two years until retirement."

"Oh shit. So, you're almost done, huh, Sarge?"

"Yep, and I can't fucking wait. Not doing a day over twenty," Delequa concluded the rant he'd wanted to get off his chest for several months now. "You need to hurry and get promoted so you can come relieve my ass," Delequa said.

"I wanna get promoted, but I don't want this job, no offense," Hines declared, adjusting his Kevlar chin strap and inspecting his MILES gear. The Army's multiple integrated laser engagement system was an overpriced laser tag apparatus soldiers wore over their gear during war game exercises. It helped Walkers adjudicate combat. If a soldier was shot in the scenario, the device would beep loudly signaling the hit.

"None taken," Delequa said, spitting a wad of black saliva to the ground, "now tell me your plan."

0450 HRS

1

Hines gave a quick rundown of the mission, and once complete, he turned and walked away from the hood of the HUMVEE with haste.

"Hey," Delequa called out. "You forgot your map."

Hines didn't hear him; being in the zone is a real thing. Hines's only focus was readying his sand table for a mission brief to his one and only surviving troop and commander. He moved with a sense of purpose through the lacy ferns that carpeted the earth.

Delequa sighed, gazing down at the map, all alone in the middle of the woods. He looked over the route discussed once more, replaying the brief again in his mind to ensure it made sense, with no glaring obstacles. Rough terrain would severely hinder the mission and their movement. He reached up and traced his fingers across the gridlines, studying it all the way to the exact grid location tasked for the team to provide an observation post, circled on the map with green permanent marker.

"Fuck me," he complained aloud. "It's gonna be a long hike."

He peeked into the front window of his truck at his cell phone, and the urge to play Candy Crush called out to him. The device sat atop a clamshell battery charger currently charging his P25 handheld radio. This super-powered walkie-talkie was the most affordable the Army could buy in mass quantities. Beside the clamshell sat two extra radio batteries, neither of them charged.

2

William Delequa was born and raised in Natchez, Mississippi. He was an only child, and his father, a factory worker, and mother, a schoolteacher, worked hard to provide him with everything he needed. Raised in a Christian home, his parents instilled a set of values in him early, but that didn't mean everything resonated with him. While attending the University of Mississippi, he made a bad decision one night, one that involved a young woman and fornication. He'd only known her for a couple hours and didn't find out she had his bastard child until the boy was eight years old. Once Delequa returned from his first deployment to Afghanistan the judge ordered a blood test and the results confirmed it: The boy, named James, was indeed William Delequa's son. The judge ordered years of back child support, which hurt William financially for years, until he reenlisted under George W. Bush and received a twenty-thousand-dollar bonus. This helped pay what he owed.

After the dust settled, Delequa attempted to build a relationship with his son, but it wasn't easy, nor would it ever be. To James, William was a stranger and his mother's sperm donor. No more, no less. Over the last few years, Delequa awoke many mornings, the reality of the situation bringing him to his knees, and he would weep. The thought of rarely, if ever, seeing his kid due to his career in the military broke his heart. He had missed the first tooth, first steps and first words even. Did they share mannerisms? Who was this young man created from his genetics?

Slowly, Delequa gave up the fight and settled on seeing James twice a year, maybe less. The fact his college fling and her husband lived in Missouri with the boy complicated travels, but the distance was just an excuse. Where there's a will, there's a way, but Delequa had neither. It was an uphill battle; one he didn't feel like fighting. It was what it was, even with his own aging parents' pleas to better the situation and enable them to see their one and only grandson. Now their twilight years filled with sadness, forever longing for things to be different. In his heart, Delequa was a free man, and he loved it, not caring what others thought. Shitty to say, but that was the truth. As he liked to say, "You can want in one hand and shit in the other. Let me see which one fills up first."

Mileage separated them. Even if the kid lived closer, Delequa had changed duty stations every three to five years. His work schedule was unforgiving with hardly any time off. There's a saying in the military that if Uncle Sam wanted you to have a family, he would've issued you one, and that statement is as true as the day is long. Eventually, distance and time kept the relationship strained. Heartbreaking, but it was nothing new to military life.

0500 HRS

Delequa's cellphone alarm reminded him to send an early morning text to his son, yet deep down, Delequa knew his son wouldn't reply, and the fact crushed his spirit. For now, James remained a foreigner.

Sadness overcame his heart, and despair beat down his psyche. Delequa looked away from the phone and rubbed his eyes violently to prevent tears from forming. Locusts screamed from the trees, producing an eerie sound occurrence for all to hear. Suddenly, the wind changed. Faster than the snap of a finger, and the air around Delequa turned cold, ice cold. Odd for a Louisiana summer morning. Delequa shook off the brisk chill, secured the map and walked from the hood, kicking up dust and clumps of mud from his combat boots. Time to snuggle under his Woobie again. As he neared the cheap green plastic door that led to his mobile tactical home on wheels, a voice rang out.

"Protect him," a distant, distorted, and unworldly voice growled from the dark morning.

Delequa froze in place, his muscles locked up like a car's brakes before an accident. Suddenly, he couldn't move, think, or breathe. The cold air deepened. The stench of decay whiffed by, sending Delequa's fingernails digging deep into the laminated map, permanently creasing the protective plastic. He closed his eyes and swayed his head swiftly from side to side.

"You're not real," Delequa whispered. "Go away."

Ferns flattened and popped as footsteps approached. Something, someone, moved closer behind him.

It was a presence Delequa was no stranger to. These encounters happened every few months or so and had been transpiring for years. Often enough that he told his psychiatrist about them, but the Army's mental health doctors aren't always the best. To the contrary, most of the time they're the absolute worst, lacking empathy or sympathy and always shoving pills down patients' throats. Getting soldiers returned to duty is their only concern. Once the soldiers return, they fear their counterparts and leadership will label them as a nut case, endlessly referred to as Suicide Steve. Delequa opened his eyes, his breath floating on the chilly air, thick as cigarette smoke. Footsteps progress across the earth and thick foliage, now ever so close.

"I said, go away," Delequa begged.

"Save him, William."

The voice terrified Delequa. It was a voice he will never forget; a voice he cherished when the individual was alive. A voice he continued to hear from beyond the grave.

"I'm no hero," Delequa admitted, tears forming across his eyes, blurring his vision. "I couldn't save you, Jason, and I have to live with that the rest of my life." Delequa cried, "I can't even save myself. I've made so many mistakes. The relationship with my son is shit. He hates me. I'm nothing to him."

"William," the voice rumbled, echoing off the bones of Delequa, "remember who you are."

A twig snaps right behind Delequa, the pressure felt through his combat boots. An overbearing and powerful presence sent goosebumps down his torso.

"I am nothing," Delequa admitted.

"To the world," the voice rattled, "we are nothing."

Snot dripped from Delequa's nostrils, falling like a cursed green rain, splattering across the earth. A harshly burnt hand with yellow bones and charred flesh crept across Delequa's shoulder. Maggots fell from the deceased, ghostly fingers, bouncing off Delequa's fatigues and onto the ground. He watched them wiggle and squirm below.

"Jason," Delequa muttered, finally able to turn, ready to face the phantom he is responsible for creating, but all that lies before him is the darkened woods.

Delequa, disappointed yet somehow relieved, longed to stand nose to nose with the specter of this fellow soldier. Jason Robertson, the teammate and dear friend who had burnt alive in Afghanistan after a rocket-propelled grenade struck his tactical vehicle. Delequa had seen his dead friend while shopping at Wal-Mart, once when getting out the shower, and on many occasions while raw dogging random women lured to his apartment from Plenty of Fish. The fear of seeing the apparition face-to-face plagued his subconscious.

Delequa collapsed to a knee and wept, trying hard not to attract any attention. He dug into a small sewn pouch on the lower half of his military trousers, struggling momentarily, and removed a bottle of pills. The yellow plastic and white label brought a change of contrast to his eyes. The bottle read: SEROQUEL.

A temporary fix for the mentally wounded and broken, Delequa popped the top and jiggled a pill free. He tossed it into his mouth, creating the right amount of spit between his cheeks to send it down the pipe, then leaned his head back like a baby-bird swallowing a worm.

0700 HRS

1

Delequa woke to the morning sun across his face. Prisms flashed and flared across his vision.

He had made it back into the truck but didn't remember how; a side effect he experienced from the medication. His iPhone rested inches away, face down on top of the blue Yeti cooler. He sat up and sucked back the drool that flowed from his thin lips.

Hurried footsteps raced through the ferns, pine needles and dead branches outside his vehicle. He cleared away the remaining saliva, pretending to have his bearings and shit together, and tried to focus with the drug still running strong in his system.

"Sergeant, where you been?" Hines asked speedily, sweat dripping from his face, dragging the camouflage face paint with it. "We've been in a firefight with enemy forces for the last hour!"

Delequa leaned forward, groggy and achy. "Huh?"

"Right after I briefed the commander, a group of G-Man hit the alpha-alpha."

"Too bad it wasn't a real engagement. You'd be dead, and I'd still be asleep."

Laughter came from Private Calhoun, now in the company of his section leader.

"We took no casualties and we're ready to step off."

"Really," Delequa blurted out, rolling over on his side and checking his watch, still heavily lethargic thanks to the meds. "It's fucking zero-seven hundred hours, and your mission brief was supposed to be at zero-five this morning, so what was the fucking hold up?"

"Timeline got pushed back. We had intel come in that enemy forces were in the area, so they put us on base defense," Hines explained.

"Exciting, now fuck off, I need more shut eye," Delequa said rolling to his stomach and pulling his Woobie over his head.

"Sergeant, no bullshit, we got to step off," Hines instructed.

Despite his body and brain telling him to sleep, Delequa dug deep and found the motivation to get it moving, even if it was at the pace of a sloth in the rainforest.

Somehow, he had escaped an ass chewing for not being present to help adjudicate the firefight Staff Sergeant Hines mentioned. Enough Walkers must've been present when the engagement occurred. Unwontedly, Delequa sat up, more like a drunken college student instead of The Undertaker this time, and made his way from the back of the vehicle. The two Soldiers stepped aside as the salty sergeant made his way to the driver side door to grab his fighting load carrier, an apparatus designed by the Army to hold several pouches for ammo, two hand grenades, bottled water, radios and first aid kits. However, Delequa's pouches consisted mostly of sunflower seeds, candy wrappers, a green notebook, and two-hand grenade simulators that had been in his possession for over five rotations. Small amounts of TNT packing enough punch to remove a hand in the blink of an eye filled the simulators. Walkers weren't supposed to have them personally; only opposing forces used them as signatures when attacking, but Delequa had always been quite the rebel. Fuck the system.

"Calhoun and I are gonna head over to the entry control point and standby," Hines informed, his voice a bit agitated.

"Ranger bat that!" Delequa energetically yelled.

Hines and Calhoun walked away, concerned at the odd behavior coming from the old crotchety soldier, and headed for the ECP, stepping over large tree branches and piles of coyote shit.

"Is Sergeant Delequa all right? Calhoun quizzed.

"He looked a little out of it, huh?"

"Roger that. He was acting strange," Calhoun asserted.

Hines glanced backward and saw Delequa adjusting his carrier, readying himself for the dismounted patrol through the wilderness. Hines reached up and squeezed the back of Calhoun's neck, much like an older brother to a younger sibling.

"He's fine," Hines said, "just saltier than my ballsack."

2

Back at the truck, Delequa quickly gathered the things needed for the movement. He put on his protective eyeglasses, followed by his black gloves and patrol cap. Delequa checked his carrier one last time and noticed the P25 radio wasn't in its respective pouch.

"Fuck me sideways," Delequa hissed.

He reached into the truck and removed the radio from the clamshell charger and shoved it into its rightful pouch. Last, he attaches the hand-microphone to the device, routing the long wire around his body and clamped the speaker onto the tiny metal D-ring loop attached to the upper right portion of his carrier. Tilting his head to the right shoulder, he pressed the button to talk.

"Eight Charlie, this is Kilo five-eight." There was no answer.

"Eight Charlie, Kilo five-eight, come in, over."

A voice emitted from the handheld radio, "Kilo five-eight, this is eight Bravo. Go ahead."

"Stan, is that you?" Delequa asked, knowing damn well who it was. He'd been a Walker for three years and knew all the civilians that supported his section.

"You know it, over."

"Hey eight-bravo, is eight Charlie there?"

A loud bleep came through after Delequa released the button.

"Eight Charlie stepped out to smoke, need me to pass anything along to him?" Stan's country voice requested.

"Nah, I'll try to reach him again in a few."

"All right, sounds good, eight-bravo, out." Delequa shoved the radio into its pouch.

"Fucking civilians," he griped.

0715 HRS

1

The two cavalry scouts arrived at the entry control point, ECP for short. The security checkpoint consisted of nothing more than five orange Jersey style barriers placed in staggering positions along a dusty and lengthy trail that led into the training area where the opposing forces waited. The ECP served as a safety measure controlling foot and vehicle traffic entering and leaving the assembly area. A team of exhausted military policemen occupied the ECP for the time being, battle tracking and letting headquarters know when soldiers left the base to take the fight to the enemy. Accountability of soldiers is one of a Walker's many priorities, and the ECP assists them in that way.

Calhoun walked to the first Jersey barrier closest to the entrance, threw his rucksack down and propped his buttocks right on top of it. Hines removed his ruck carefully, placing it at his feet to make a last-minute adjustment to the shoulder straps. A military policeman pulling security with a machine gun from behind a set of trees observed the duo.

"Alright, Domino's, Pizza Hut, or Papa John's?" Calhoun asked, "You can only eat one the rest of your life."

"Oh, Pizza Hut," Hines proclaimed. "Hands down, they're the best."

"Damn, I took you more for a Domino's guy, sergeant."

"Nope."

"Okay, okay," Calhoun rushed, "Fuck one. Kill one. Marry one."

"This ought to be good," Hines said and cut a handsome grin.

"Jane Fonda, Nikki Minaj, and Beyoncé."

"That's a terrible list, Calhoun."

"Well, that's the list."

"Damn," Hines pondered, running a quick, demented scenario through his mind. "Alright, I got it."

"Send it, Sergeant."

"Kill Jane Fonda. Fuck Nikki Manaj. And marry Beyoncé's rich ass."

"She's got all those kids though," Calhoun clowned, "and you gotta deal with Jay-Z's punk ass."

"I'll whoop Jay-Z's ass first time he steps foot on my porch," Hines jested, "then I'll bring his old lady upstairs and eat her ass."

"You'd eat her ass, Sergeant?"

"Hell yeah!"

"What's wrong with y'all white people," Calhoun cracked.

Both soldiers laughed hysterically, attracting attention from a cluster of artillery troops conducting personal hygiene several meters away. Shaving cream covered the onlookers' faces. Half-assed constructed lean-tos and ponchos hung between the trees and their big guns, both a poor attempt at cover and concealment, and at detouring potential rain. The lone military policeman looked away from the scouts and resumed pulling security.

Hines countered with a distasteful tale. "True story. Before I married my wife, I was dating this freaky chick all about ass play. One night she slammed her index finger in my ass while she was blowing me! I nutted so hard my fucking legs locked up and my goddamn pinky toe went numb. Thought I was having a seizure."

"Good Lord," Calhoun declared, slapping his legs like an old-timer hearing a tale, "I'm gonna piss myself!"

Above the laughter and jokes, the sun revealed itself from behind a fresh set of clouds. Soon the heat would sweep across the state of Louisiana, making the wet, summer morning humid and dank, miserable for all souls.

A moment later, Delequa arrived at the ECP fully befuddled and vexed, his face advertising a man sick of the job, maybe even his life, and there was truth in his demeanor. Under the disdain for the job, he had to bury the hate, soldier the fuck up and execute.

"All right, ladies," Delequa spit, moving his hands across his body performing a final preparation check of equipment, his face still under the influence of medication. "Time to work the nastiness out of our bodies."

2

The pair glanced at one another and slung their rucksacks to their backs. Calhoun's held a portable FM radio for communication back to the battalion assembly area, but it hadn't worked the entire rotation. It was the teams' only link to higher command if they could get it working. They inserted magazines into their weapons, locked and loaded with blank ammo, and stepped off from the control point. The men wove through the grime-covered barriers and loads of concertina wire strung across the jagged woodland trail that led into the assembly area of soldiers.

Staff Sergeant Hines removed a green compass from his pocket and wrapped it around his neck. He had bought it years ago after reporting to Fort Benning. It swung from side to side as he maneuvered the uneven trail, accompanied by a topographical map tucked snugly in his cargo pocket. Private Calhoun followed his leader, reaching into his upper sleeve pocket to remove a pack of Marlboro Lights and lit one up, never falling behind. The group pressed on.

Upon entering the box, a lone soldier stood guard alongside the entrance. He issued a brotherly wave to the travelers, all of whom returned the wave, apart from Delequa, who followed close behind, stumbling along the rough terrain.

"Eight Charlie, Kilo five-eight, over."

This time, a twangy voice is quick to respond. "Go ahead, Kilo five-eight."

"Roger, stepping out on a dismounted patrol time now. Two personnel en route vicinity of Khushal to establish a listening post and observation post for early warning detection of enemy forces. I'll call once we arrive, over."

Again, a quick response, "Hokey-dokey, don't get lost, over."

Keen to close out the transmission, Delequa pressed the button to transmit.

"Ranger that, Kilo five-eight out." Transmission ended.

Delequa followed close behind the soldiers, blending into their shadows as they left the assembly area. In the wake of the urgent need to push out to the observation point, he realized he had left the two extra radio batteries next to the black clamshell holder in his truck. Forgetfulness was another extreme side effect of the medication, as well as with PTSD which now plagued him daily. Delequa knew piss poor planning always led to a piss poor performance.

Part Two:

THE STAR-CROSSED LOVERS

1100 HRS
15 August 2017

1

Deep in the government-owned timberland, Ava Munn, a newlywed and proud member of the Deridder Lions Club Auxiliary, could hear her husband's sweet words piercing through her subconscious. She wanted to answer but found herself lost in total darkness.

2

"Open yer eyes, Princess," Kurt whispered, sweetly running his fingers through his wife's dirty-red hair. "I need ya' to wake up."

Kurt Munn was Ava's husband of less than two months. A local bad boy from the small, blue-collared town of Leesville, Louisiana, fifteen miles north of Deridder, and only two miles from Camp Polk.

He had the reputation of a party animal to everyone living in Vernon and Beauregard Parish. To some he was a loudmouth, to others he was a hilarious jokester. Voted class clown in high school, and usually the first to throw punches in a bar-room brawl. People either loved or hated his reckless antics. To local law enforcement, Kurt was a certified troublemaker and repeat offender with a rap sheet to prove it.

He spent a part of his youth in juvie hall up the road in Alexandria, sentenced for small theft and vandalism, but by the time he hit his twenties, DUI's plagued his record. Kurt's lost his license for a year, forcing him to sober up for a while, but not for good. Old habits die hard. He craved the bottle like a Catholic priest's thirst for young altar boys. No one blamed Kurt for how he turned out. His father, Jacob, was an infamous drunk and womanizer while his mother, Nancy, was a sex-obsessed country girl that favored the dark meat, and neither were worth a pot to piss in.

Growing up, accusations always swirled that his mother rode cock for cash. With earnest concern, he brought up the rumors one day and received a soul crushing face slap that buckled his knees for an answer. They were never close. He learned to cope not by defending her honor but countering with his own "Yo' mama" joke. When his mother died in a car accident on the way to Lake Charles in 2008, Kurt hadn't mourned her death. The wake at the funeral parlor reeked of formaldehyde and cheap perfume on the inside. Kurt came to blows with his father outside. A well-placed uppercut sent Jacob flying into the Magnolia bushes that welcomed visiting mourners. There he lay, flat on his back, snoring, the scent of whiskey apparent to all. After the incident, Kurt never spoke to his father again. Life had dealt Kurt a white trash hand from the start. Until the night he met Ava.

A mutual friend introduced them at Club Zydeco in Leesville, and they had hit it off. One thing led to another, as they often do, and what had started as a one-night stand ended with Kurt not pulling out. The "L" word blossomed thereafter and came up in conversation. After a four-month whirlwind, they moved in together. Mere weeks later, over heavy margaritas, Kurt proposed on bended knee, offering his commitment of eternal faithfulness in the parking lot of Buddy's Seafood. His friends told him he was crazy, but Kurt didn't give two shits about what they, or anyone else had to say.

He was in love.

Really, he was.

Ava, shot by the same dastardly, arrow-wielding cherub, foolishly agreed to take his hand in marriage. Love is a powerful drug and Ava was madly in its grip.

Word quickly spread around town that her parents wouldn't approve, but there wasn't a damned thing they could do. Once her parents found out about Kurt's small-time criminal record and DWI's, his presence alone physically sickened them. Family dinners were awkward meals eaten in silence. Never would there be a pleasant moment with the in-laws. They believed she deserved better, and truthfully, she did, but Ava was young, dumb, and impassioned. Trying to convince her otherwise was an impossible task. As the saying goes, "Young, Dumb and full of Cum."

The lovebirds tied the knot at the Leesville Courthouse, a gorgeous piece of infrastructure built in 1871 during the height of the timber industry, and notably the best spot in town to get hitched. Scenery suffered in the area and lacked establishments worthy of hosting such memorable events.

Leesville isn't everyone's cup of tea. The people of Wal-Mart provide local entertainment, sporting colorful, toothless meth addicts and mullet rocking cowboys on the daily.

Right before the lovers entered the Judge's chambers, Kurt promised Ava he'd give up drinking. At first, she didn't understand why he made the promise, because drinking wasn't an issue. Hell, they founded their relationship on booze and bad decisions. She shrugged it off, but that promise Kurt made came from the purest part of his heart.

But that turned out to be a lie.

Everything happened so fast. Deep down, Kurt wanted to be good for her, despite not knowing how. Giving up drinking was his way of doing that. He wanted to change something about himself to prove his love and commitment to her. In the end, his demons would end up getting the best of him.

Soon, his unexplained late nights and emptied bank account prompted verbal altercations between the two. Their love now exposed as mere infatuation, it soon faded as fast as it began. At least for Ava.

1105 HRS

1

"Open yer fuckin' eyes you cheatin' ass whore!" Kurt growled.

He smashed his fist into Ava's jaw and her eyes flickered. All she could see was blackness. A throbbing pain radiated from her jawbone, her body heavy, aching, and uncomfortable. She felt as though she was leaning over a precipice, close to falling, just hanging on. Her eyes opened, pupils rolling behind her eyelids, still only darkness. The blistering summer heat made its way across her freckled body. Sweat flowed from her face down to her navel.

"Why are my tits so hot?"

Ava realized she was naked; butt naked, like the day she was born. The sun projected its anger down her slender shoulders. From the direction the heat met her flesh it must have been around noon, but she couldn't figure out why she was outdoors or why she couldn't see. A light summer wind blew past, caressing her bare skin, causing her nipples to retreat inside her large light-brown areolas. Her youthful breasts were large, and perky firm.

Suddenly, a finger traced around her nipple, either to arouse or molest her. Seconds later, lips latched on, sucking violently like a famished baby. She struggled to fight off the sexual assault, rocking her body back and forth, trying to get away. A rough material secured her shoulders, midsection, and hips with ankles spread eagle to the sturdy base of a towering tree. The assailant continued to suck her breast ragingly, painfully. The burning sun returned, momentarily taking her mind off the assault, until the tit-sucking violator bared teeth, sending a sharp pain into her armpit.

"St... stop..." Ava cried out.

She twisted her upper torso and yanked her shoulder blades backwards, attempting to remove the nipple from the assailant's mouth. In doing so, she caught the strong scent of hay, reminding her of a rodeo show.

It was the rope. She grew up smelling it.

2

During her childhood, Ava traveled to see her Uncle Charlie every summer. He lived in Robert, Louisiana, a small settlement ten miles past Hammond and four hours southeast from Leesville. While visiting her relatives, she would help with farm chores. Her cousin, Barb was always her favorite to hang out with. Barb would jump up and down on the front porch, screaming at the top of her lungs as Ava's car pulled into the driveway. That sight always made Ava laugh. She would exit her parents' vehicle with a backpack full of goodies and pictures from the previous summers visit in tow, as the girls locked hands and ran giggling, already gabbing about New Kids on the Block. Before their feet made it to the first step of the porch, Donnie was the subject of conversation. He was the member they both crushed on the most. To finish the day off, they would head over to the rope swing tied to an old oak tree, where various family members swung them so high their hearts dropped inside their chests. The feeling of adventure and excitement never got old, and Ava loved it.

The adults encouraged the kids to play in the yard, inside the barn a fair distance behind the house, and in the pasture with the grazing horses. They were never to play in the woods - ever. The adults didn't explain why, and it wasn't until Ava was older that she found out the true reason. Turned out, during those summers on the farm in the early 90s, three young boys had escaped a satanic cult intent on sacrificing them to the devil. While traipsing on the rope swing with her cousin, drinking cherry Squeezits, Ava was unaware of the wickedness and cruelty that existed around her. Once she discovered the truth, the reality sent shivers down her spine.

Yet despite the demons and dark secrets throughout the world and specifically in southeastern Louisiana, riding along the woodland trails on horseback was always the highlight of her visits. Family members loaded the horses into trailers before dawn, and the trucks headed down to the gas station on HWY 190 to fill up before making their way to the entrance of the Bombing Range.

During World War II the acreage northeast of Robert served as a gunnery range for pilots intending to head overseas and bomb Nazi scumbags with warheads on foreheads. After the war, however, the land became the main location for trail riders. It was a region of land riders dreamed of, outside of the unexploded ordnance scattered throughout the range. It would've been a shame for a horse and its rider to hit an active thirty-pound bomb buried beneath the earth, but no one seemed to give a shit. If it was your time to go, it was your time to go.

The men saddled up the horses while bitching about their wives and their lackluster sexual performances, finishing the first twelve-pack of the day before mounting their trusty steeds. The women loaded up the band wagons with kids too young to ride and ensured they placed enough hay across the wooden floorboards to comfort their rear-ends. The ladies bitched as well, nagging as they worked, mostly about their husbands' small peckers and paychecks. They tied down blue and red coolers in the far corners of the wagons, filled them with juice for the little ones and booze for the Coonasses and Rednecks, who drank enough by ten o'clock to take on an indigenous force via fisticuffs.

For miles on end, they rode, chatting, laughing, drinking, and breaking in new horses purchased from the livestock exchange in Loranger. On one such occasion, Uncle Charlie, in all his wisdom, put Ava on an unbroken horse. It was a small horse, a Shetland pony to be exact, and Uncle Charlie thought nothing of it, as Ava was a decent rider. Boy, did he regret it. He was as wrong as the red bird fucking the blue bird for putting her on that animal. Turned out the poor bastard was blind. The horse kept running off the trails through thick lush green woodlands at breakneck speeds with Ava in tow, screaming for the good Lord to save her life. Uncle Charlie chunked his beer and broke away from the trail to rescue her from the dark brown Shetland, *Ray Charles* as they later dubbed him. This happened many times. It was scary each time the horse got away, galloping and crashing through brush, but it was Ava's favorite memory from those times with her distant relatives, and her favorite story to tell friends back home in Deridder. The smell of rope, leather, and animal became forever ingrained upon her senses.

1107 HRS

1

"*Why am I naked? Who's sucking my tit? Am I going to be raped?*"

She licked her numb and dry lips nervously. It was like licking concrete and the thick iron taste of blood endured on her tongue. Her thoughts came clouded, and her jaw continued to throb with pain. She was naked, confused, aching, and scared. Panic made its way into her. She turned her head frantically from left to right attempting to regain her vision, but only darkness greeted her. She attempted to jolt herself loose again, but it was pointless; she was not going anywhere. The assailant detached from her nipple and stepped back.

"Wakey wakey, eggs and bakey," Kurt rhymed.

"Kurt... honey... is that you?" she questioned.

A tailgate slammed down, startling her. She rotated her head in a circular motion like a kid lost in a fun house. Kurt reached into the back of his red 2012 Nissan Titan and shuffled a set of heavy black duffle bags. It was an expensive gas guzzling piece of shit with a cockeyed *HILLARY CLINTON* presidential campaign sticker on the left side of the chrome bumper, fading under the harsh Louisiana elements. Kurt was a dumb, southern Democrat and always would be. Just another poor, uneducated liberal bastard.

A red-cockaded woodpecker, Louisiana's favorite tree driller, hammered away into a pine in the distance as the trees surrounding the couple swayed together with the passing breeze, a much-needed relief. Summer was in full swing, and the humidity was not fucking around. It grew hotter by the minute. In her mind, Ava wished it was winter. In Louisiana, the winters are typically low thirties in the morning, high fifties by lunch and back down into the thirties by night. Today, winter wasn't coming, and it was hotter than Satan's garage.

"Kurt, answer me, please. You're scaring me! Where are we?" she pleaded frantically. There was no reply.

"Answer me!" she screamed. Every animal in the Kisatchie National Forest heard her plea.

1109 HRS

1

Kurt stepped away from the duffle bags and strode over to the thick longleaf pine where he had secured Ava. The same tree he bowhunted from every year. His favorite hunting spot was one of the few safely guarded secrets he kept even from his wife.

Ava, bruised and powerless, listened to the sound of grass shuffle beneath her husband's feet as he approached. Kurt glanced down at her stubbly vagina. He missed it, almost as much as he missed her big tits. The couple hadn't fucked in weeks, well, at least not each other, and Kurt missed the warmth of her velvet insides. Her tight orifice clenching around his member was a pleasant memory he desperately desired. Reaching up to Ava's forehead, he yanked off the thick blindfold that covered her face.

Her eyes, sensitive to the sunlight invading her weakened pupils, pressed tightly together. She raised her eyebrows high and tried to ease the sensitivity in her corneas. Kurt grabbed her face, pressing his lips against hers. His breath reeked of devil water. *Jose Cuervo*, Ava's most cherished beverage on nights Kurt requested anal sex.

The action bewildered Ava. She closed her eyes tight, wiggling her eyeballs frantically against the back of her eyelids, hoping it would help in regaining her vision. Kurt shoved his tongue into her mouth, running his hand over her pussy and pinching the labia together with his fingers. It hurt worse than the vicious tit sucking she received earlier, but this time she didn't resist. As her mind raced, small squeaks of discomfort escaped her lips as Kurt released her fuck flaps and removed his mouth from hers. Ava opened her eyes; her vision was still fuzzy but returning. She gazed into her husband's bearded face resting inches from hers. There was madness in his eyes.

"Go ahead, bitch. Look around," Kurt said, menacingly.

Ava did as instructed. Her heart pounded so hard she could feel it between her ears. With haste, she surveyed the area, starting with the ground, wiggling her toes to ensure they were all there. Her toes dug into the dirt. Beads of perspiration dotted her entire body as streams of thick sweat flowed from the center of her chest down to her lean, sexy hips. Tears filled her eyes.

"What the hell is going on?"

She peered over Kurt's right shoulder, her neck aching and stiff, and saw Kurt's truck, Red Rhonda she liked to call it, parked several feet away. The tailgate was down, and empty Rolling Rock beer cans congregated in the filthy bed, along with clumps of dirt, dried paint, and grass trimmings from the lawnmower Kurt borrowed a few weeks ago. A shovel lay next to two duffle bags, and against the back window atop the Kobalt toolbox was the half-empty bottle of Jose Cuervo.

2

Ole Jose always gave her enough liquid courage to meet the demand. Once the foreplay had wrapped, she would assume Kurt's favorite sexual position, Doggy Style. She would place the pillow under her face so the neighbors wouldn't hear her moans through the poorly insulated apartment walls and readied herself. With her ass raised upward, Kurt would spread his saliva across his hand and run it over his throbbing cock. Ava rubbed her clitoris vigorously to stimulate pleasure before Kurt slid his penis inside her anus.

Getting the tip in was the worst part, but after two thrusts, it wasn't all that bad. The pain eventually went away, and she didn't understand why more women wouldn't try it. At the same time, she didn't understand why she must always get drunk first.

Kurt liked to spread her ass-cheeks apart and stare at his dick sliding in and out of her. It was a major turn on. Ava continued to masturbate to climax, and when she came, she'd squirt her victorious juices onto the bed sheets. Every so often, she gushed. For most men, Ava was a sexual unicorn; an erotic creature diligently hunted. A carnal partner men craved to experience, at least once. A squirter.

Even after scientific studies discovered the clear liquid released during orgasm was diluted fluid built up from the urinary bladder, basically piss, men still yearned for it. They wanted to experience the phenomenon.

She didn't squirt every time, but when she did, boy, it was a mess for Kurt. Cleaning up after intercourse got old real fast and the laundry detergent bill continued to rise each pay period, but he never admitted to her how he truly felt. He didn't want to embarrass her, and he knew she couldn't control it. But in secret, deep down, he grew to hate the squirting. That shit got old quick.

However, on the more romantic nights when Ava and Kurt climaxed together, the sex was exquisite. Always a nice way to promote intimacy, and the mess didn't seem to bother him then. In those moments, he showed pure affection and wholeness, which was important to a relationship intended to last forever.

She always felt closest to him when dual climax occurred, but after the honeymoon phase, their love started to fade, and so did intimate sex. That is when Ava began looking for love in all the wrong places, and she found it. No man had ever busted her guts as hard as Denis Hallberson, her secret lover.

1111 HRS

1

A

va looked away from the truck and surveyed the wooded locale, making note of a well-travelled dirt trail wide enough for vehicles to the left of the clearing. Hopefully, if she could free herself, the trail would lead to a main road, allowing her to find the way home.

Again, the woodpecker laid into a massive pine, sending echoes of its work throughout the woodlands, and solidifying her location. Kisatchie National Forest is where most of the woodpeckers reside. The state blocked off certain portions of acreage to help the endangered birds thrive and flourish. If anyone were caught by the Game Wardens hunting or even parking their vehicle close to a tree marked with three white lines, a hefty fine would follow.

"The forest- yes, I'm in Kisatchie Forest."

But the forest was massive, and she had no clue of her exact location. Chunks of dried mud and deep gashes inhabit the earth around the clearing, either from teenagers mudding and fishtailing, or from heavy armored military vehicles from The Box.

"Is it hunting season yet? How deep in the woods am I?"

Through her thoughts, she heard the faint sound of whooshing blades. Throwing her head back against the tree, she focused on the skyline above. Kurt stumbled backwards following her gaze into the gorgeous light blue summer sky.

A UH-60 Helicopter flew over the clearing at a high rate of speed. The Army's primary and most versatile rotary-wing aircraft, there hasn't been a conflict the chopper didn't take part in. Panama, Iraq, Afghanistan, and of course, Somalia, from which the movie *Black Hawk Down* made the utility helicopter famously known throughout the world. Many countries across the globe have their own version of the helicopter, but none are superior to the U.S. Army's.

The big iron dragonfly zipped across the sky. Ava caught a glimpse of a red cross painted on the belly of the chopper. With a flash, a large explosion erupted, so powerful it shook the Nissan Titan, sending the bottle of *Jose* falling from the toolbox and smashing to pieces in the truck bed. They both felt the impact though the blast was miles away.

"Motherfuckin' shit!" Kurt yelped, throwing his hands across his face as if blocking a boxer's punch.

"Argh!" Ava cried, closing her eyes once more and bringing her chin to her chest.

Kurt stumbled to the tailgate, grasping for balance. *Jose Cuervo* officially taking hold. He gathered his dignity and walked toward the drivers' side door, opening it.

"Fuckin' Army fags always blowin' up shit out here. Fuckin' government lap dogs, baby killin' pieces of shit. They think they're better than everybody, but they ain't shit! Ain't that right muthafucka'?" Kurt cursed the heavens.

Ava began to cry, the stress becoming too much, and her large breasts wiggled and bounced in unison with her sobs. She opened her eyes, keeping them fixed to the ground, too scared to look at her deranged husband.

"Kurt, who are you talking to, honey?"

Tears rolled down her pretty face, but Kurt didn't respond. Instead, he leaned against the cab of the truck, head tilted towards the sky. Then Ava's heart fell into the acid of her stomach.

"Denis..." she whispered.

2

Trussed to the pine across from Ava was Denis Hallberson, a Staff Sergeant in the U.S. Army and native of Columbus, Georgia. Thirty feet separated the once secret lovers. Denis was also nude, not positioned spread eagle like Ava, but bound at the position of attention with multiple ropes interlacing over his entire body with far more rope than it took to secure Ava's one-hundred-and-forty-pound frame. The bruised flesh of his torso signaled his broken ribs, and a burlap sack covered his head. Ava didn't need to see his face to know it was him. There was a tattoo on his chest, a sacred heart with the name *HEATHER* emblazoned beneath that gave away his identity. Ava had gazed upon it many nights while making love to the gentleman who preferred sex in the missionary position. She had no clue *who HEATHER* was, and it doesn't matter now. The affair is out of the bag, and she would probably never find out. She glanced down at Denis's crotch and cried out.

"Oh, my God! Kurt, what are you doing?"

Kurt had tied a knotted string at the base of Denis's swollen, flaccid penis, cutting off circulation to his impressive member. Denis's penis, a good eight inches when erect, now lay inflamed, rocking dark purple and puffy skin. Engorged and ruptured dorsal veins protruded from the proud appendage.

1118 HRS

1

The truck's engine breathed life, emitting a low rumble, and Kurt removed himself from the cab, placing a hand below the window to keep himself upright as *Jose Cuervo* brought the fight to him.

Leaving the door open, he moved back to the tailgate, tightly clutching a new bottle of devil water in his hand, and propping it against the latch assembly. He struggled to unzip one of the duffle bags.

"Open up you sum-bitch!" Kurt swore.

With one last yank, it opened, spewing the smell of gasoline. Ava broke down, tears constantly flowing.

"I'm... so sorry... honey," she sobbed.

Kurt removed a chainsaw from the bag and slammed it down on the tailgate, chipping away small pieces of paint. Ava could hardly speak and despite the heat, her body felt cold.

"What's that for, Kurt?"

"It's for you and ya' cocksuckin' boyfriend over there," Kurt said, pointing at Denis, "and guess what?"

A gaze of utter terror was her only response.

"There ain't nobody round' here to hear y'all scream." "Kurt..."

"Stop sayin' my fuckin' name, Ava! You weren't sayin' it when you was fuckin' Mr. Soldier Boy over here. Why the hell you sayin' it now? You destroyed our marriage. And for what?" Kurt asked, shrugging his shoulders while taking a sip of booze, "for that no good motherfucka' right there? Mr. Big Dick Soldier Boy? The man that enjoys fuckin' other men's property."

"Honey, please, let me...."

"Stop! Don't fuckin' say shit, whore. Shut yer mouth! It's too late. You can't fix what ya' done. Ya' hurt me, Ava! Ya' hurt me real bad! Ya' were the love of my life!" Kurt yelled.

Ava continued crying.

"And now, I'm gonna hurt ya,' in every way I can. I would've done anythin' for ya.'" Kurt bit his lip, fighting back the pain of betrayal. "I tried, ya' know, I really did. I'm not perfect and neither are you, but this is unforgivable, Ava, and yer gonna pay for it."

Her woes disappeared. Anger, as hot as the day was bright, gave her the courage to speak.

"You're a drunk, Kurt! You're a goddamned drunk, just like your father! I'm miserable with you. I never pictured my life turning out this way. We live paycheck to paycheck, constantly worrying about our finances and we never have money for anything. We didn't even have enough money to buy my tampons last month because you drained the damn bank account! I should've listened to my folks. My dad was right about you!"

"I said shut the fuck up!"

"No, no, I will not! I will not shut up! You need to calm down and listen to me," Ava instructed.

"We're past the point of me calmin' down, woman."

"Damn it, Kurt. Please, just talk to me!"

"No!"

"You've lost your mind!" Ava screamed.

"I haven't lost my mind. I've lost my wife!" Kurt's thunderous voice echoed throughout the wilderness, temporarily de-escalating the situation.

Denis remained lifeless through the argument.

"You haven't lost me, Kurt. I'm still here," she stated, her voice sweet.

Kurt disregarded the statement, reaching back into the duffle bag. Hushed whimpers emanate from Denis. Ava's heart pulsated with extreme anxiety.

"He's waking up. He must break free and save me. I know he will."

Kurt removed a small handheld blow torch from the bag and inspected it. Ava's eyes expanded, almost like insects,' and the heavy crying returned. The maintenance equipment was old and dated. Kurt fiddled with the control knob and a hissing expelled as he squeezed the trigger. Bright blue gas-fueled flames mixed with orange and red exited the torch head.

"Yet," Kurt replied, "I haven't lost ya' yet, but I will. I promise, this'll be over soon. Time to wake yer' boyfriend up," Kurt sneered.

He slammed the blowtorch down, walking from the tailgate to the driver's side door again.

"Denis! Denis! Wake up!" Ava commanded.

"Nookie," from Limp Bizkit's album *Significant Other* sounded from the interior. Kurt adjusted the volume, looked down at the pump-action 12-gauge shotgun resting on the floorboard, then exited from the vehicle.

"Shit," Kurt remembered.

The jam blared as he re-entered the cab, opening the center console. Empty Copenhagen snuff cans and miscellaneous trash fill the plastic compartment, but underneath the garbage lay his BUCK knife, shiny with an orange stabilized wood handle.

"There... that's better," Kurt said, stumbling toward Denis, knife in hand, malice burning bright from his eyes. Funky bass lines and a solid drum beat power a soundtrack for horror.

1120 HRS

1

"No, Kurt, no!" Ava bawled.

"Awake yet, soldier boy?" Kurt shouted.

Denis squirmed, showing signs of life as Kurt positioned himself next to his prey. He slapped the bound man across the face and grabbed his testicles.

"Can ya' get hard for her now, soldier boy? Huh?" Kurt fondled the two large, hairy round orbs.

"Stop it! Stop it!" Ava ordered.

Kurt released the testes, spitting in his right hand and spreading the lube over Denis's penis. Then he began stroking it.

fap, fap, fap, fap

A surge of sadistic vengeance overtook Kurt. He spat in Denis's face and dropped the knife. The soldier's cock remained limp, showing no sign of life. Ava observed the act with outright disgust. Kurt jerked her lover's cock harder. Lethargic moans radiate from Denis's semi-conscious body.

"Yeah, ya' like that, queerbait? Come on now! Show me what ya' got, soldier boy!" The tugs turned even more vicious as the foreskin reddened and ripped.

fap, fap, fap, fap

"Want them balls pulled on, big boy?" he inquired.

"Stop it now! What's wrong with you?!" Ava screamed.

Kurt pleasured Denis with one hand and stretched his testicles with the other.

"Arghh...Arghhhh!" Denis wailed.

"Finally, some participation. Scream, you wife fuckin' piece of shit! Scream, boy!"

The noon day heat was now unbearable, a special kind of warmth only Louisianans truly appreciate, and the vigorous volunteered masturbation was giving Kurt an unwanted workout. And his murderous attire wasn't the best idea he had had on the day, nor was it the worst. A long-sleeved, Buffalo Plaid flannel shirt, jeans, and cowboy boots.

Beads of sweat rimmed his brow as he yanked the enemy's scrotum; the man responsible for ending his marriage, the man who had felt the warmth and tightness of his wife's pussy. He released Denis's ball-sack and retrieved the knife. Dust projected from the blade as he placed it to the base of Denis's shaft.

"Ugh... aargh..." From underneath the burlap sack, the awakening confusion turned to terror. Denis shook furiously, feet digging into the earth.

Ava looked to her spouse while Denis fought the inevitable. Madness filled Kurt's eyes, once gorgeous green pupils filled with love and desire. She realized now the heat of passion and wickedness consumed him. Maybe, just maybe, she could reach him. But he would have to listen to her, and that didn't seem to be an option. Not now at least. Everyone has a breaking point. A point of no return, and Kurt was straddling the point where logic and sanity refuse to co-exist.

The woodpecker hammered away again as Kurt focused on Denis, licking his lips. He made the first cut.

2

Kurt elongated the penis as the knife gashed it open. Denis's muscles bulged as he squirmed, screeching to high heaven, held firm in the position of attention.

"Such a good little soldier," Kurt teased.

"Oh my God! Oh God, no!" Ava shrieked.

Kurt cut through the urethra allowing dark-yellow urine to evacuate. Dorsal arteries drizzled blood; circulation had stopped hours ago. Small drops of blood speckled Kurt's hands, but quickly washed away courtesy of the piss oozing across his knuckles. Kurt gagged but continued to sever.

The smell of piss reminded him of spewing vomit into a urinal at the bar while shit faced.

Denis's urine reeked to holy hell due to dehydration. Tendons separated and popped as the pecker was close to removal. Screams racked Kurt's ears and concentration. It motivated him to cut faster. Half a slice later, Denis's manhood separated. Kurt grasped it tight, ensuring it didn't fall to the ground, and for the first time all morning, he felt an emotion other than anger.

Confidence.

To complete the job, Kurt cut away the remaining string around the penile shaft. Dark blood squirted in all directions as the rest of Denis's bladder emptied, much of which landed on Kurt's boots and jeans. He stepped back, admiring the emasculation.

"Look honey," Kurt joked, "he's a squirter just like you!"

He raised the detached penis, like a prized war trophy for his wife to see, flopping the cock around like a dog's chew toy.

"Please, somebody help us! Please!"

"I said shut up, whore!" Kurt emphasized.

Denis's cries of pain pierced the chaos. Kurt yanked the burlap sack off Denis's face.

His eyes a reddish brown, they sparkled and displayed a hypnotizing gaze. Kurt almost found him attractive. Almost.

Denis is a better-looking man than Kurt, and at one time had a bigger dick too, but that's not the case anymore.

"Ya' got somethin' to say to me, soldier boy?"

"Please..." Denis grumbled, his voice high and hyper. "I have a family... a little boy... and a wife."

"A wife?" Kurt asks surprised, "Does yer' wife know ya' fuckin' my wife?"

"No... she doesn't... know."

"So, ya' have a wife, but she doesn't know yer' fuckin' my wife. Interestin'. What's her name?" Denis didn't answer; instead, he looked to his slam-piece, Ava.

"Ava... I'm so sorry."

"I said, what's her fuckin' name?"

Kurt rammed Denis's penis into his mouth, shoving it in as far as he could. Denis tried to combat the assault. Kurt pushed the severed member further down his esophagus. Veins bulged in Denis's neck and vomit erupted from his mouth, bypassing the phallus blockade, sending several chunks into Kurt's opened mouth and beard.

"Ew... fuck!" Kurt protested.

Denis's eyes watered from gagging and heaving, but Kurt forced it deeper.

1126 HRS

1

"Stop it, Kurt!" Ava pled.

At the sound of her voice, Kurt snapped out of his murderous, suffocating rage. He retracted the prick from Denis's face and threw it at Ava as hard as he could, losing his balance in the process. The cock wobbled through the air, missing Ava outright and landing several feet behind her.

A horrible throw if there ever was one.

Kurt had never been the athletic type and hadn't played a lick of sports growing up unless you consider backyard brawls a sport. He fell to his knees, exhausted like a pitcher in the ninth inning of a game and regurgitated an ungodly amount of white, brown, and yellow bile. He wiped the saliva and upchuck from his bushy lips, swaying on his knees and looking skyward to the calming and stunning atmosphere. Kurt didn't notice, but he'd planted both knees firmly in Denis's pool of excrement, now drawing in an onslaught of flies ready to feast.

Ava tilted her head down, trying to chew through the rope fastened across her collarbone, but her teeth could not find purchase enough to bite. She gave up quickly; not much fight left in her.

"Why? God, why? Please, I beg of you!"

"Fuck! Fuck!" Kurt spit. He stood up, wet circles surrounding his knees.

"Please, Sir. I beg of you. Please let me go. I don't wanna die."

Kurt turned to face Denis.

"Well, well, soldier boy ain't so tough now, are ya'?"

"Please... Please," Denis whined.

"Ya' know what?" Kurt asked, slapping his hand firmly to his hip, "Maybe I'll go introduce myself to yer' wife when I'm done with ya', how'd 'ya' like that, hero? I can go play Daddy for ya'?"

"Please, don't hurt my family," Denis stressed.

"You hurt me! And ya' destroyed my marriage! I'll never have a family now!" Kurt roared, face bright red, "And after I get done playing Daddy with yer' boy, how about I take yer' wife beneath the sheets and fuck her brains out, huh?"

Denis didn't respond; his mind struggled to keep the horrible thoughts at bay. "Now, let's try this again. What's her name?" Kurt asked, unforgivingly.

Denis leans forward.

"Heather," he huffs, "her name is Heather."

Denis's handsome face now displayed failure, defeat, and extreme dread. For Ava, the news broke her heart. Now she knew who *HEATHER* was, and the truth hurt more than anyone would ever know. She was a fool; a damned fool, played by a man with a family.

She hadn't seen it through the heavy lust and excitement. Denis had a family. A life, a wife, and a son. They should've been the loves of his life, and weren't, but neither was Ava. She was nothing more than a side bitch, fuck of the month, truth be told.

"After I slide my dick inside yer' wife, Heather, since you can't anymore," Kurt teases, "I'm gonna nut all up in her pussy, and maybe, I'll finger fuck her asshole while pulling her nipples until they touch the bedsheets. Ya' be okay with that?"

Denis remained silent.

"Do ya' know what it feels like to stand before yer' woman, ya' wife, knowin' another man has been inside her? Knowin' he's felt the insides of her warmth and she's felt the thickness of him? Do you know how that feels? Yer' woman, the one chosen by God to be yers forever; the one destined to be with ya' the rest of yer' life and despite yer' mistakes, despite ya' biggest flaws, she's the one who's supposed to stand by ya' until your dyin' days. Do ya' know what that feels like when that special someone gets ripped away from you, Denis?"

"No," Denis whispered.

"Now, think about this," Kurt paused for dramatic effect. "One day, you hear a rumor goin' round town that yer wife is screwin' a soldier boy from Polk, so ya' follow her around one night and find out she does in fact have a fuck-boy, and man, the reality really sets in then, brother. The rumors aren't rumors anymore, they're truth, fact. A fact that slaps you right in yer fuckin' face. And once ya' realize she's not in love with you anymore, yer heart jumps out yer chest. Pain is all you know. Ya' feel like you're dyin'. Drownin', and just the mere thought of her bein' with another man makes you wanna die." Kurt paused again, spitting on the ground. "Then, my dick-less friend, ya' become a laughin'stock, a source of gossip in the town. And you know Leesville and Deridder ain't that big, so everybody wants to talk 'bout it. Yer buddies tell ya' yer not man enough to keep a woman by yer side and ya' let someone take 'er away from ya'. See, I had to do somethin' about it. I won't be made the fool. It's the principle, Denis. The principle." Kurt explained.

He lifted the knife up and placed the tip of the blade on Denis's forehead.

"Ahh..." Denis shrilled.

"Now, let me let ya' in on a secret. Let me present ya' with some facts," Kurt said, staring directly into Denis's eyes. "Yer' gonna die today, fuck-boy. Yer' gonna pay for what ya' done. And that cunt over there, my precious wife," Kurt said, removing the knife from Denis's head and pointing it at Ava, "Her no-good cheatin' ass is gonna die too. But first, she's gonna watch what I do to you, because she's gonna get it ten times worse."

"No! No!" Ava wailed, "By God, Kurt, please, don't! You can't do this! I'm your wife! We can walk away from this. We can fix this, honey, I promise! I promise you!"

"Liar!" Kurt screamed, placing the knife to Denis's throat.

"Nobody's walkin' away from this. Not even me," Kurt confessed. "Yer' dead to me, bitch. Soon to be nothin' more than a bad memory."

Ava peered into the bulging eyes of a madman.

Denis sniveled as the blade pressed into his skin. A light stream of blood flowed from under the silver blade. Once the song ended and Limp Bizkit exited the scene, the sharp knife would start slicing. All the lights inside the truck flickered and faded. Odd, but no one in the clearing paid mind to the truck.

"You can't do this, Kurt!"

"Watch me!" Kurt declared, bringing the knife high into the air.

"Denis!"

"Ava, tell..." A flurry of stabs prevented Denis from speaking his last words. The attack rained down in a series of blows that were fast and furious, fueled by bitterness.

Kurt knew there was no turning back, and resentment compounded the assault. Denis screamed bloody murder as the penetration wounds bled heavily, bright red blood flowing like the Caddo River. Kurt continued to stab away at the defenseless man. Furious jabs peppered the center of his bare chest. A forceful blow struck Denis's shoulder, peeling back the dermis of the skin revealing bone.

Out of breath, Kurt rested, hands on his knees. Ava turned her head as far away as she could and screamed.

"Help me! Someone! Anyone! Help me!"

Shrubbery rustled in the distance, attracting her attention. Desperately, she focused on the area.

Something had moved through the foliage with haste. Snot dripped from her nose, her shoulders and chest were now completely sunburned, and all she could do was cry out.

2

With a blood-curdling scream, Kurt returned to his onslaught. The first blow delivered a massive stab to the trachea, and dark blood instantly spurted from the wound. The phonatory muscles destroyed, Denis's screams are no longer a concern for anyone. Propped up like a good soldier, he had no choice but to receive his punishment. Kurt was the alpha and the omega: the beginning and the end.

"Denis!" Ava squealed.

The next blow struck the edge of his collarbone, deflecting the knife's path downward, removing a nipple.

"Fuckin'... Piece...Of... Shit..." Kurt ranted, stabbing away. Subsequent lacerations reached as far as his naval.

"I'm... done... with you!" Kurt cursed, turning and throwing the knife deep into the woods. The onslaught was over.

Denis bled from all parts of his torso yet remained conscious and alive despite heavy blood loss. He gurgled and wheezed as blood bubbled, frothed, and popped around his lips with each breath. Gore covered Kurt's face. In a trance, he made his way back to the bed of the lifeless truck.

"Denis..." Ava grieved.

Kurt paid her no mind as she mourned the lover that stretched her vagina wide. Kurt grabbed the chainsaw.

"Ya' know, I didn't think I had it in me. My whole life I've been nothin' but a joke to myself and the people of this Podunk town," Kurt admitted. "You're supposed to be the one that fixed that. I believed in ya' and ya' made me start believin' in myself."

"Kurt, please," Ava beseeched.

"I loved you so much, Ava. Ya' were my heart and my everythin'. I would've died for you. You know that, right?"

"Yes, yes, Kurt," she agreed.

"Good," Kurt said, placing the chainsaw on the ground.

1133 HRS

1

An object crashed through the bushes not far behind Kurt. Ava heard it and searched for the cause. It sounded like someone had thrown a baseball into the impenetrable foliage.

"Who's there?" Kurt asked. His voice nervous, shaky for the first time today. His body maintained a good defensive posture, as his heart pounded with grim intent.

Ava scanned the area, hoping and praying that *someone* would save her.

Kurt scoured the area frantically with his eyes. "Is someone there? If so, come on out. I promise I won't hurt ya."

Nothing. Dead silence, aside from Denis's shallow breaths, amplified by the sudden tension. Each breath rattled as his lungs filled with blood.

"Come out you fuckin' coward! I know someone's there!"

"Please, help me!" Ava's voice rang out.

"Shut up," Kurt said, shaking his fist.

"Please, I know someone's out there! I can feel it! Please! Help me!"

"Zip them dick-suckin' lips, bitch!"

"Fuck you, Kurt! Fuck you!" Ava growled, sucking back a huge amount of mucus that had been accumulating in her throat. She discharged a blotch of green and white saliva from her mouth that landed on Kurt's flannel shirt. "I hate you; you piece of shit! I hope you fucking burn for all eternity!"

"I warned you, woman!" Kurt shouted. He moved away from the chainsaw and reached into the truck bed, securing the blow torch. Ava's demeanor changed in a flash. "Don't even! Stay the fuck away from me, Kurt! Stay away!"

Kurt shielded the blowtorch, tinkering with the knobs.

"Help! Please," Ava prayed. "I know someone's out there!"

"I told yer ass to shut the fuck up too many times, whore! You wanna make some noise, then let's make some motherfuckin' noise."

"Stay away!"

Animosity and pride were in full control of Kurt as the torch head spit fire like a handheld dragon. Ava bashed her body against the tree in an effort to flee, but the ropes only dug deeper into her irritated flesh as tree bark leapt from the pine.

"Time to close ya' up, princess. If I can't have you, no one will," Kurt declared, squatting down in front of his wife.

"No! Get away from me!"

Before Ava could brace for the pain, the flame blazed across her inner thigh, instantly blistering the skin and emanating a charcoal-like smell. Ava issued a dreadful cry of agony and shock. The pain was unbearable.

"Kill me! Kill me!" Ava urged.

Kurt ignored her; he was on a mission to maim and mutilate, and his payback was far from over. He dragged the flame over Ava's clitoral hood. Screeches of torment satisfied him. He smiled as he rotated the flame in a circular motion over her clitoris, burning it away. A sulfurous odor clung to

Kurt's nostrils as the flames scorched away remaining stubs of pubic hair. As the scene transpired, Kurt developed an erection.

Darkness consumed him, birthing an evil within him; an evil all men on earth possess. Ava's entire upper genitalia melted under third-degree burns, right before his eyes. Kurt cut off the torch and stood up.

Mission complete.

"There," Kurt announced happily, "that ought to teach ya' a lesson, bitch."

Kurt swung forward slapping her across the tits forcibly enough to knock a grown man out cold.

Through the abuse, terror, and ungodly pain, Ava endured it all. Her throat was raw from screaming, and her body twitched and jerked from the shock of overwhelming brutality. The smell of wet tuna and burnt pork permeated the air.

1136 HRS

1

Kurt tossed the blowtorch to the ground where it rolled underneath the truck, coming to rest behind the left front tire. Kurt inserted his foot into the rear hand guard of the chainsaw for stability, knelt and pumped the primer bulb. He wanted to ensure it came to life with only two pulls of the cord.

The word *STIHL* ran along the silver bar of the chainsaw. Rusty links on the saw chain told a story of neglect, and the front hand guard was loose, electrical tape securing the handle in place. Thick grime congealed within the small squares on the white housing, and it had a cracked fuel cap. The faded instructions were barely visible. The machinery had known better days. Today it would do a madman's work. Kurt adjusted the choke, looked up at his wife, and grinned.

"Ain't love grand?" Kurt pulled the ripcord, the chainsaw rattled.

False start.

Kurt pulled harder, this time the chainsaw rumbled hungrily to life. He quickly adjusted the choke and squeezed the throttle. Black clouds of smoke exited the monster's exhaust; it's roar both intimidating and promising instant death.

Ava lost hope. The end was surely near. She tried to scream, but only managed a few faint squeals before passing out, as though her soul had left, gone to a place of dreams. Kurt raised the chainsaw, emulating a Tusken Raider, and unleashed an absurd scream. It disappointed Kurt that she would not witness him ripping her lover to shreds. The feeling only pushed Kurt further over the edge.

The chainsaw revved, as Kurt looked to his rival; the man responsible for all of this.

Kurt's facial expression mirrored lunacy. Time for the kill.

He sprinted towards Denis like a locomotive, the chainsaw emitting a constant roar that left behind a cloudy black trail of death. There was a slight kickback as the tip of the chainsaw met the upper portion of Denis's stomach, but nothing Kurt couldn't handle.

2

When Kurt Munn was a young boy, he worked in a timber yard in Pickering, Louisiana with a group of hard-working folks that spent much of their time clearing trees for Camp Polk's training areas, hauling pines to and from the lumberyard. H.B. Thompson was the name of the company, but it had been sold off and renamed. Kurt earned a lot of experience behind a chainsaw working for them. They taught him precision with the wood-eater. Specifically, a man named Danny Dantona mentored him. A big, burly, hardworking dago from Robert, Louisiana, the same place Ava spent her summers.

It was hard work, but Kurt didn't mind. He enjoyed the labor because it kept him away from home. And when his muscles were sore, at least he was feeling something. Love and affection had never existed in his life until then. He always knew he would not amount to shit, but hoped one day that would change. He was an incurable romantic since watching *The Princess Bride* at thirteen. He always wanted someone to save him like Wesley saved Princess Buttercup, but his future never seemed that bright. A whore mother and drunken father is all Kurt ever knew, and ever would until he left home.

Beatings from his father, Jacob, came daily, while his mother, Nancy, fucked strangers out behind strip clubs off HWY 171 and Catfish Crossing, a popular local Cajun buffet. At least until someone burned it down in 2015. That someone had been Kurt.

Jacob, usually drunk driving, always brought Kurt along to help search for his mother on her late-night rendezvous. One night, around three o'clock in the morning, they noticed a lone F-150 parked in the back of the Catfish Crossing parking lot. The light poles in the back didn't work, so it was always a place to find the desperate and horny trying to get their rocks off.

The F-150 was rocking, as they pulled the shitty Dodge RAM up next to it. Kurt turned white as a ghost as he gazed upon his mother's ghastly ass rising and falling upon an enormous black man's cock. White secretions and foam surrounded her pussy, thick enough to lather your face and shave with. Kurt distinctly remembers the man's hands spreading his mother's ass cheeks so far apart that he could see the discoloration of her asshole.

It was an image that would never go away, ever. An image that kept him a virgin until he was twenty-three. Kurt realized that night what his mother was and what she did all those nights she went missing. This led Kurt to burning the fucker to the ground. A shit buffet that provided cover for a shit-ass mother and her sexcapades.

Burn baby, burn.

Having to accept your mother as a slut and your father as a worthless drunk wasn't easy and Kurt dropped out of school in the tenth grade. Besides, there was always good money in the logging business. They paid him under the table until authorities discovered his crime and sent him to juvie. Once released, H.B. Thompson refused to take him back. Kurt returned to Leesville, jobless and depressed with nowhere to go. He refused to return home. No way in hell was he going back. He contacted old friends and found places to crash, promising he would get his shit together. It was almost Kurt's nineteenth birthday when life dealt him a lucky hand. He got a maintenance job with the railroad. The work wasn't as strenuous as logging, but it kept him busy. He repaired and extended tracks all the way up into Zwolle and sometimes up into Shreveport, and although he enjoyed the job, he never forgot his skills with a chainsaw; the insatiable wood-eater.

1140 HRS

1

Kurt leaned his weight into the saw and opened Denis's stomach right up.

"Full throttle motherfucker."

The chain spun faster than the eye could see, removing chunks of flesh in a hurry. Kurt gripped the front hand guard tight and squeezed the throttle. Flesh and blood ejected from the bottom of the blade, hitting the bumper spikes as intestines fell to the ground below. Wave after wave of blood mixed with innards soaked Kurt's clothing. The slaughter reeked of burnt muscle and gasoline.

Kurt shoved the blade further in until the saw penetrated the tree, bogging it down as it ground through bone and wood. Denis's body shook, like a bolt of lightning surged through him. His mouth slacked open, drooling thick, dark blood. Perfect circles of blood splattered the pinecones scattered across the earth. Kurt rerouted the chainsaw upward past the lower level of the sternum. This reminded Kurt of hunting season and the last doe he gutted, ignoring the gore that now drenched his hairy face.

"Kill. Kill. Kill. End this fucker's life."

By the time the blade pushed through the upper sternum, Denis was dead. His hollow carcass still stood at attention, held by a few remaining ropes. The key position for all stationary facing and marching movements; such a good little soldier. His torment was over thanks to Kurt's cruel rage. A massive pool of blood surrounded the base of the tree.

"Die, soldier boy!" Kurt ordered triumphantly.

Kurt released the throttle, and the forest fell silent. As quickly as the terror started, it ended. Kurt jerked the chainsaw out of Denis and stepped back to admire his work. With a broken mind, all Kurt saw was red; his vision swirled with malice. For the first time, Kurt absorbed what he'd done.

The horror. The death. The murder. The mutilation. He stared upon the body of a husband, soldier, and father, but felt nothing. Absolutely nothing. Not even hate. How odd.

2

There was one left to go: his wife, the whore. After he finished with Ava, he'd use the shovel to bury the bodies. If he couldn't have her, neither would the coroner; she'll remain in a shallow grave well-hidden and forgotten. After that, he'd blow his brains out with his granddad's shotgun. The shotgun collecting dust on the floorboard of the truck will be his last F-you. Kurt refused to be taken alive. He was in control now and suicide was the only way out. Kurt had a plan, and it was a good plan.

The chainsaw ran idle hanging freely at his side, blood dripping from its gnarly teeth. His forearms were sore and fatigued, but he felt accomplished as exhaustion blanketed his body.

"Ava..." Kurt called, "Look at what ya' done made me do." She remained asleep, dreaming of summers in Robert accompanied by psycho killers in the woods.

"Ava!" Kurt yelled. He brought the chainsaw back into full swing with a squeeze of the trigger, sending black smoke into the atmosphere. Kurt approached his wife, both hands gripping the chainsaw.

Time to take out the trash. Precision is key.

Part Three:
THE LUMBERJACK, THE WOMAN, AND THE SERPENT

1015 HRS
15 August 2017

1

The soldiers navigated through the forest for hours, reshooting azimuths and stopping for piss breaks. The landscape was full of Tupelo Gum trees that grow ninety feet high. The long march angered Delequa, sending rage coursing through his veins, but he kept his composure. He was drenched head to toe in perspiration from drudgery. Despite the exhaustion and frustration amongst the troops, the sergeant played his role. Being a Walker wasn't always sunshine and rainbows. At one point the team questioned if they were lost, having no sense of direction and lacking land navigation skills, but like a good soldier, Delequa allowed them to progress without saying a word.

"I wish I had my cellphone so I could call us an Uber," Calhoun fantasized.

"Cell phones aren't allowed in the box by rotational training units, bud," Delequa interjected, "so if you have one, you better hand it over before a bigger asshole than me catches you with it. I've seen UCMJ action taken against troops that brought them in the box."

"Don't fret. All our cell phones were locked up and stored back in a connex in Alexandria, Sergeant," Hines informed.

"Good," Delequa declared, "I have one in case of emergencies so don't worry. And no, you can't use it, gentlemen."

"Why can't we have cellphones though?" Calhoun asked.

"Are you gonna have a cellphone when you're in a fire fight with the Chinese?" Hines quizzed.

"I might if they got Verizon over there."

Hines released a chummy chuckle as he passed through thick brush.

"Spoken like a true millennial, kid," Delequa chimed in, secretly impressed by the young soldier's response. "But you don't have a fucking cellphone because we train in the same fashion as we will be fighting. That's the problem with your pussy-ass generation and the Army. You want everything your fucking way, and life just isn't like that. Someone is always lowering the standards for the next generation of soldiers to serve in the Army. Pathetic," Delequa spit. "In my opinion, the last great generation died face down on the beaches of Normandy."

Calhoun chewed on the response for a minute but said nothing.

"Quit running your ball-washer and pissing Sergeant Delequa off, Calhoun." Hines instructed, "Keep moving."

"Roger that, Sergeant," Calhoun agreed.

2

Along their trek, the soldiers crossed narrow cricks, bypassed wetlands, and dared treacherous greenery without thought of injury. The life of a soldier is an adventurous one, and marching was a dreary task often filled with *No Shit, There I Was* stories that rivaled any tall tale told by the average man or woman in the civilian sector. Despite the hazards, the team carried on, refusing to allow the Louisiana bush to defeat them.

"Are we close to Khushal, Big Sarge?" Calhoun asked, panting.

Delequa stared back coldly.

3

Calhoun slapped his neck hard, instantly killing one of the unidentified bug species the wilderness proudly called a resident. In the dirty south, there are many undiscovered insects and creatures, many of which seemed to be out in full force against the observation team. Pressing forward, the group made their way down a steep ridge infested with Loblolly pines and Laurel oaks that supplied needed shade. Downwards they marched, steering through native Louisiana bottomlands.

"Fuck this state," Hines complained. "I don't know how people live here."

"The heat ain't the worst part," Calhoun interjected, "The politicians get that medal!"

"Politicians?"

"Yep, the most corrupt motherfuckers in the country all have office seats here," Calhoun exhorted,

"And they don't give a fuck about what happens to the state."

"How so?"

"The same carpet's been in the New Orleans airport since I was ten years old. They've never changed it. It's an embarrassment to the state."

"Oh yeah, I forgot you were born and bred here."

"Roger that, Sergeant," Calhoun admitted. "Unfortunately, I am. Joined the Army to get away from this state but look at me now."

"Same stains on the carpet, huh?" Hines pondered, "I can believe it."

"Yep, and if you only knew the money the state makes off tourists during Mardi Gras it'd blow your fucking mind. We could've rebuilt the ninth ward after two Mardi Gras seasons, but nope, the city still looks like shit, and people remain in poverty."

"The goddamn city shouldn't even continue to exist," Delequa finally spoke, yards behind the team but close enough to listen in on the conversation. "One day it'll be underwater like Atlantis, and when that happens, I'll move back to this shithole state and start a treasure diving boat tour."

"That's one way to make a living," Hines said.

Calhoun snorted, visualizing the reference.

"I bet motherfucka's be finding all kind of waterlogged dildos along Bourbon Street," he joked.

"You'd find them scattered around Marie Laveau's house of voodoo for sure. That's my turn around point on bourbon," Delequa said.

"Yeah, those gay clubs be running hard after Laveau's," Calhoun admitted.

"Can't say *gay*, Calhoun," Hines instructed. "It's triggering and will plant your ass in the First Sergeant's office faster than your two-mile run time."

"You for real, Sergeant?" Calhoun asked, nervously.

"Yep."

"Now there ain't nothing wrong with anyone being gay," Delequa declared, "I don't judge folks. I don't think anyone wearing this uniform does," he paused, feeling pride in his heart. "Neither of you gents have to worry about offending me," Delequa stated. "People need to stop being so goddamn sensitive." He swatted at a swarm of gnats. "That's the problem with the world. Thank God this generation didn't fight World War II, because we'd all be speaking German and shoving bratwurst up each other's asses."

Both scouts chuckled at the graphic commentary. Twigs and branches snapped as they maneuvered through a patch of thorn bushes.

"I could go for a bratwurst right about now," Hines joked.

The team chuckled, and for the first time, Delequa smiled.

4

Being a black man in America isn't easy and growing up in the ghetto down past Plank Road in Baton Rouge wasn't easy either. Reggie Calhoun had always dreamed of a different life, but it wasn't a change that would occur overnight. The ghetto was a concrete jungle that hosted notorious acts of violence alongside drug dealing, and many of Reggie's friends did not live to see their mid-twenties. By age nineteen, Reggie figured there wasn't much time left if he didn't make those changes in his life quick, fast and in a hurry. His life had been hard. It was the only life he'd ever known, but he understood it didn't have to be that way. The streets were unforgiving and dying with a crew that really didn't give two shits about him, or his family, or the dreams he wanted for himself, was unappealing. Reggie hated the idea in fact, so he did something about it.

He wanted out of the gang. No more repping red bandanas with matching attire. He knew no one ever left the gangs; at least not alive or without a severe ass kicking and trip to the Huey P. Long hospital. They didn't say *Ride or Die* for nothing.

One night after stealing a shit ton of Tommy Hilfiger clothing during a snatch and grab score in the Cortana Mall, Reggie noticed an Army recruiting station next to the exit as he fled Mall Security. That was the day his plan materialized. After the heat died down, he returned to the mall and visited the station, took the ASVAB and scheduled a visit to MEPS. After receiving a good bill of health, he was scheduled to ship off to Fort Benning for Basic Combat Training in less than three weeks. He never told his immediate family or gangbang buddies about his plan, but he told his cousin, Jamarcus Williams, a Sheriff's Deputy out in Hamily, Louisiana.

The day finally came to ship off to basic, and Reggie left the world he so desperately wanted to escape. It happened in the blink of an eye. Without warning family and friends, his recruiter picked him up from the Krispy Kreme Donut shop on Plank Road under the cover of night and before he knew it, he was on a plane bound for Atlanta, ready to face whatever adventures lay ahead. When family realized he was gone, they called everyone except the President, asking about his whereabouts. Reggie's mother called Jamarcus begging for help, but he gave none and spoke nothing of Reggie's situation.

Over the next few weeks, Jamarcus secretly provided Reggie the encouragement and motivation needed to finish basic combat training. His cousin's opinions and advice were all that mattered since leaving Baton Rouge, even to this day. Reggie hadn't returned home and had no intention to. Life in the Army was good, despite all the crazy ass white folk that served within the ranks.

5

"You guys wanna hear a war story?" Delequa asked, his mood more pleasant from the comedic banter, despite the intense warmth of the day.

A trail of sweat ran into Hines's ear hole, and he quickly wiped it away. "Hell yeah," Hines exclaimed. "Anything to keep my mind off this heat."

Calhoun leapt over a small stream that ran downhill into a huge pond visible further to the west. "I love old-timer stories," he ribbed, casting a grin over to Hines.

"I bet you do, Calhoun," Delequa wisecracked, "Ya' little bitch."

The Cavalry scouts snickered. Sergeant First Class Delequa eased the tension with his witty personality, a side of him he hadn't let them see, but it was a much-needed change to help motivate the troops.

"Anyway," Delequa quipped, rolling his eyes like a schoolgirl, "On my second deployment to Afghanistan, my team was out in the middle of nowhere manning an overwatch of a small village, when suddenly, we're told to break down and establish a checkpoint between two mountains we called Darkside and Berico. The battalion commander wanted us to search for a potential bomb maker that was using one of the mountain passes close by to transport his explosives and shit." Delequa popped another serving of tobacco into his mouth without slowing a step. "So, we broke down and moved to a road between the two mountain ranges, rugged territory, you know, and reports came to us from higher up stating the bomb dude had a big, ugly ass mole on the inside of his right thigh."

"A fucking mole," Hines giggled. "How the fuck did someone know that?"

"Shhhh, let him finish, Sergeant," Calhoun hissed, holding back chuckles. Hines looked back with a smile running from ear to ear.

"Fuck if I know," Delequa admitted, "But we sat on that checkpoint gazing at every Bedouin's cock and balls for two full days."

"Holy shit," Calhoun squeaked, barely holding it together. "Did you find the mole?"

"Hell no," Delequa confessed, spitting a wad of tobacco on the ground. "That mole probably never existed, but we got to see some of the driest, nastiest, anteater dicks of all time. Those peckers haunted my dreams for weeks."

Hines cackled as amusement erupted, halting the tactical movement. Calhoun stopped dead in his tracks and wiped tears from his eyes.

"It wasn't my finest moment in life," Delequa acknowledged.

Hines leaned forward at the waist, gasping heavily from laughter. His smile was infectious. One thing Delequa had learned over the years, no matter the situation or circumstance, soldiers always welcomed a good boost of morale.

"I just wanted to share that story since we were discussing dicks earlier, and no matter how shitty the mission or day is, much like our little stroll today, we embrace the suck and execute."

"That's the truth, Big Sarge," Hines said.

The troops pushed on.

1055 HRS

1

After bypassing the thorn bushes, the soldiers regrouped and assisted the removal of spikes from their uniforms. Hines brought the map to the ground and examined it. Once done, he stood up, brought his compass to his cheek, gazed through the aperture, and shot another azimuth. So far, they'd travelled only two miles, a klick short of their original grid. Calhoun removed his radio and extended the antenna from the rucksack. After pressing numbers on the preface, he put the hand microphone to the side of his face and pressed it firm against his ear to perform a radio check.

"Ghost 7, this is Ghost 2, radio check over."

Throughout the march, Delequa had checked his cellphone sporadically to track their movement with GPS, ensuring they didn't head into an impact area where demolition and live projectiles detonate. The app had been the best ten bucks he'd ever spent. Using a compass was a dying art, and why do it if you didn't have to? So far, the pair had stayed on track, and by Delequa's mental calculation, they would arrive in an hour or two, depending on the terrain. Boy was he ever ready to take a knee.

"Any station to this net, this is Ghost 2, can you read me, over," Calhoun challenged.

No response.

2

"You got any children, Staff Sergeant Hines?" Delequa pried.

"No, not yet," Hines said, adjusting his azimuth.

Delequa stepped away from the sun's wrath to the shade of an old willow oak growing on an incline. "You want kids?"

"Yeah," Hines admitted, lowering the compass from his cheek, "I do."

Delequa returned a small nod. The question was too personal. For individuals to have a successful military career moving up the ranks, they must learn to be lonely at the top. And loneliness wasn't something foreign to Delequa. Men who served in Panama, Kosovo and Desert Storm, men who did violent and unspeakable things during their time at war, these were the mentors that had molded and heavily influenced Delequa's leadership style. Always keep it professional. Never let it get personal. Care for your soldiers and lead them, but don't get too close.

Old timers believed fraternization was the key to destroying the integrity and discipline of the Army. If the popularity of mixing work and play got in the way, the big green killing machine would fail. Likership would replace leadership, and all would be lost. Therefore, the leaders that raised Delequa dealt in absolutes, much like the Sith. Everything was black and white with no wiggle room. No fucks given to who liked them. You are not here for subordinates to like you; you're here to do a fucking job. When in charge, be in charge, and only socialize with your peers to avoid favoritism and resentment between team members. The only thing that mattered was the mission.

Over the years Delequa had never really found a peer that he connected with. No close friends were made. Many associates were nothing more than backstabbers looking for ways to climb the promotion chain. Yet deep down William Delequa wished it wasn't that way. A part of him wished he could get to know Shelton Hines outside of work. Getting to know the man on a personal level would be quite the honor. Delequa knew his heart was pure, but old habits die hard, and Delequa was set in his ways, even though sadness and the yearning for friendship always had a room reserved in Delequa's heart.

"Do you have any kids, Sergeant?" Hines asks, flipping the question.

"I do," Delequa admitted, rubbing the sweat off the back of his neck, "but it's complicated."

"Complicated," Hines picked, "I thought complicated was your middle name, Big Sarge."

"Funny." Delequa said coarsely.

A small, shit-eating grin escaped Hines's lips. Delequa turns to walk away from the magnificent willow oak but didn't get far.

3

A resounding presence breathed through the wilderness, an auditory noise only Delequa heard. His line of sight followed the sound to the top of the hill above the group where Jason, his old teammate, stood between two massive pine trees. Instantly, his blood ran cold. Jason stood motionless, head tilted to the side, smoke wafting from his charred uniform and carbonized, skeletal face.

"Please," Delequa mumbled, "leave me alone and go away."

The deceased soldier remained, projecting dread, shame, and regret, all of which Delequa already felt for the phantom invisible to a sane soldier's eyes.

"Sergeant, I can't get nobody on the radio," Calhoun stressed.

Hines was re-plotting grids on the laminated map strewn across the ground. "Communications are shit out here, haven't worked since day one. Don't stress it. We're about a mile out," Hines stated, standing up. "We'll try to reach them again when we get there, let's keep moving."

"Sounds good, Sergeant," Calhoun replied, disassembling his FM radio and stuffing it into his ruck. Hines drank from his canteen and noticed Delequa staring into the distance, unengaged.

"You all right, Sergeant Delequa?" Hines asked, screwing the top back on.

No reply.

Delequa stood frozen in fear, not knowing if the apparition he gazed upon was real, or a figment of his imagination. Maybe, somewhere along the way, he'd gone crazy, or maybe it was God's way of punishing him for his sins. Delequa knew everyone would answer for their shortcomings.

"Big Sarge," Hines spat, snapping his fingers loudly.

Again, Delequa didn't move or acknowledge the section leader. Calhoun threw his carryall across his back and adjusted the straps under his armpits. Hines, ready to complete the movement, walked up the incline to Delequa and pulled the back straps interlaced across his shoulder blades.

"Sarge," Hines said calmly. "Big Sarge, you're freaking me out."

"Do you see him?"

For the first time since the deployment, the unnerved survivor of the Afghan war acknowledged the spirit of the dead. It released a fleeting relief across Delequa's spirit. Concerned, Hines searched the woods, unsure of what he might find. Abruptly, the woodlands fell silent.

"See who, Sergeant?" Hines inquired.

Delequa brought his face a fingerbreadth from Hines's cheek. "Between the two pines, look again, atop the hill."

"Did you see an animal?"

"Just look goddamn it," Delequa instructed, keeping his eyeballs glued to Hines's face.

Hines did as told, aiming his vision between the pines. He squinted, straining to see what the Sergeant alleged to be present. He identified nothing, not even a squirrel. It occurred to him that Sergeant First Class Delequa might have untreated issues.

"I see nothing, Sergeant."

"Nothing?"

"Not a goddamn thing," Hines maintained.

Questioning his sanity, Delequa looked back between the pines. To his relief, but no surprise, Jason is gone. Vanished once more to the realm of afterlife.

"Watch out Sergeants," Calhoun bellowed, "Snake!"

4

Both Sergeant's heels lifted high, bouncing around like two juicers at a winery sharing a basket full of berries. The copperhead, one of Louisiana's most dangerous foes and a master of camouflage, elongated his body to issue a dose of poison into Hines's veins. Thanks to Calhoun's early warning, the serpent's fangs struck the bottom of Hines's combat boots, sending the reptile into a state of panic, tumbling down the crest of the incline back towards Calhoun.

Delequa fled in the opposite direction, sprinting like a jackrabbit. Maybe the apparition that stalked him was a thing of evil with intentions of destroying his sanity. Maybe it wasn't a coincidence; perhaps Jason was responsible. Perchance the copperhead was a *form* of Jason, manifested on earth in the physical form of a sneaky *nope rope*. Delequa's mind raced with absurd thoughts.

"Holy shit!" Hines squealed, "did y'all fucking see that?"

"Close call, Sergeant." Calhoun agreed.

"Jake the Snake almost took me out," Hines spit, exhaling a sigh of relief. Let's get moving."

5

Shelton Hines was a running back from Reseda, California, the same place made famous by the fictional character Daniel LaRusso. Hines graduated high school in 2002 and attended the University of Southern California on a football scholarship. He thought he'd resume his position at running back, due to the record setting statistics he had recorded at Reseda High. Instead, he was repositioned to cornerback. His coach saw promise in him as a defensive player, but that hope faded fast. A few weeks into practice and his knee blew, a career ending injury that ripped away the scholarship he had earned, sending his ass back to Reseda. Like any warrior, admitting defeat was hard, and his parents refused to let him sink into the slumps.

It took six months for him to recover enough to resume training. He hit the gym like a madman, strengthening his body, preparing for basic training. If he couldn't play football, he'd use his physical attributes for an even more demanding job. An occupation only one percent of the United States population ventured into. His grandfather served in the Korean War and was the first man Shelton admired, even over his father. Serving in the military was a thankless job to the unappreciative. But to the citizens that truly understood the sacrifice of putting one's life on the line for others, it was the most rewarding job a man or woman could have. And as his grandfather often told him, "Only two people have ever died for humanity: Jesus Christ and the American soldier. One died for your sins, the other for your freedom, and in today's world, people are so free they fight to take rights away from themselves. Until you experience the world through a soldier's eyes, you'll never know how lucky you are to be in the home of the free and land of the brave."

Being a soldier was Hines's first dream as a youth, and it never fully faded away. His USC days would never come to fruition, he knew that and could live with it. Shelton Hines was an All American, and for the first time, felt the part.

After graduating basic combat training, his first duty station was Fort Carson, Colorado.

There, he met the love of his life, Carrie Marcell, a Chili's waitress and hardcore San Francisco Forty-Niner fan. Brought together from their reverence of football, love blossomed for all to see. They tied the knot just as Hines received orders to report to Mannheim, Germany for a three-year tour.

The years in Europe flew by. Before they knew it, they were back stateside, ready for the next phase in life. Success drove both, Carrie earned a degree in occupational therapy and Shelton continued molding himself into a phenomenal leader, one respected and admired by peers and subordinates alike, the epitome of the non-commissioned officer corps. A fearless chief, earning two bronze stars for valor during his deployments to Iraq and Afghanistan.

All Shelton Hines wanted was to complete this rotation with his troops at JRTC and return home to his wife. She'd be ovulating when he returned, and both decided now was the time to start a family. Bringing a little one into the world was something they both wanted more than anything in the world.

1107 HRS

1

The group came to rest at the bottom of a natural depression, stomachs growling with hunger. They had eaten nothing since stepping off and now was the time to refuel with only a kilometer left to go. Delequa dug into one of his pouches and stuffed his mouth full of sunflower seeds, a good source of salt and protein to keep the body moving. Hines and Calhoun found a spot on the ground and tore into their MREs, scarfing down the slop preserved in the durable pouches.

2

Residents of Louisiana weren't fans of the MRE during Katrina or the massive storm system that dropped twenty-five inches of precipitation per day during the three-day flood of 2016. People disliked their often-bland taste and lack of variety. Additionally, the perception that they were unhealthy or processed can also contribute to negative attitudes towards these types of meals. The storm flooded and destroyed thousands of homes. Cities and towns disappeared underwater.

The National Guard responded to the flooding, the nation's bastard soldiers, issuing supplies to displaced personnel. Louisianans appreciated their work, and their efforts didn't go unnoticed.

3

Soldiers in the field consider MREs a five-star meal, worthy of dining on a first date. Especially the packs boasting jalapeno cheese spread. Grown men and women fix bayonets against one another to acquire the concentrated, yellow cheese of the Gods. To say each meal was incredible would be a lie, but soldiers will never understand why civilians hated the government issued meals so much. They tasted just fine to most, exquisite to some.

4

The spiking of a woodpecker echoed through the backcountry, and Hines looked skyward to find the bird busy at work.

"That little guy is better protected than our borders," Hines observed.

"Sure is," Delequa confirmed.

"How much further, Sergeant?" Calhoun asked, leaning forward with his rucksack high on his shoulders for relief. "I'm fucking smoked."

Unexpectedly, a woman's voice cried out to the world, distant, but clearly audible.

"Answer me!"

The soldiers looked to one another, confused, unsure of what they heard. The red-cockaded woodpecker flew away from the reverberating scream. Pinpointing the location and distance from which the voice came would be difficult, particularly due to the way sound traveled in the timberlands, but it was close enough to spook the animals.

"Did y'all hear that?" Hines asked.

"Shhh," Delequa hissed.

The crew muted and listened, examining the sounds of the deep woods. A minute of silence passed.

Calhoun spoke, "Big Sarge, was that a woman?"

"I think it was." Delequa responded.

"Any idea which direction it came from?" Hines asked.

"Up the hill," Delequa suspected, "same direction we're heading."

"Really?" Calhoun said, inspecting the target.

"Check your map Sergeant Hines," Delequa requested. "I'm sure an impact area is close by, and we don't need to stumble into that."

"Hell naw, we don't want that," Calhoun admits.

"Fuck it, let me check the grid on my phone. I have an app."

Delequa broke the role of observing coach trainer and whipped out his cellphone. The screen displayed a missed call from James, and for a second, Delequa thought to call him back, but the groups safety took priority. No one wanted live rounds dropped on them due to an inaccurate grid. Delequa had let the Cavalry team play the game so far, plotting their points and executing dismounted movement, which so far had been strenuous, but successful. It was time for Delequa to ensure they were safe.

5

The application loaded, slowly but surely. The best service provider for the Walkers was AT&T, but Delequa had Sprint, a less than stellar service to rely on in the box. Delequa zoomed in on the icon that displayed their location, noticing an impact area less than a kilometer away. For a split second, Delequa questioned why he hadn't paid more attention during the migration. Part of him didn't care, but as always, the soldier in Delequa did the right thing.

"Okay, we need to head south," Delequa pointed. "I'll continue to check our location as we move to ensure we don't explode."

"Thanks, Sergeant," Hines said, relaxing.

"Play stupid games, win stupid prizes, and I don't want to win a death certificate today because I let you jackasses walk us into a live fire range."

"We'd appreciate that," Hines said.

"Sergeant Hines ain't gotta worry about the rounds, he's gotta worry about the reptiles," Calhoun gagged.

"If you weren't seconds from becoming a heat casualty, I'd smoke the balls off you, Calhoun," Hines cracked back.

The whirring of heavy blades seeped across the heavens, sending heads craning skyward.

1111 HRS

1

A

UH-60 helicopter ripped through the atmosphere, a red cross proudly displayed on the belly. It was the symbol of saviors. A massive detonation followed that sent the soldiers down to their bellies in fear of indirect fire.

"Shit!" Calhoun exclaimed; debris covered his lips as he hit terra firma. The group took cover, waiting for any further detonations.

"Told you we were close," Delequa stated.

"Too close," Hines agreed.

All three men lay on the ground in a near perfect circle, their faces staring at one another.

"Let's get to that fucking grid," Delequa demanded.

The team stood, no response needed, both wanting to get to their destination alive. As they rose, a man's tone cursed the sky.

"But they ain't shit! Ain't that right motherfucka'?"

The words low and muffled, like neighbors fighting through an apartment wall.

"Who the fuck is out here?" Hines enquired, squatting down to a knee.

"Let me make a call," Delequa suggested, walking away from the group and turning his radio down with a twist.

"Eight Charlie, Kilo Five-Eight, over," Delequa radioed.

The response is energetic and sarcastic.

"Good to hear from you, Five-Eight Kilo. We thought you died. Y'all reached your destination yet, over," the twangy voice quizzed.

"Not yet, I need you to do me a favor, break," Delequa released the button and waited three seconds. "Can you find out if any other rotational units are in the vicinity of our current grid, over."

"Sure can. Send me the grid, over."

"Roger, grid as follows, break." Delequa swiftly opened the app on his phone and focused on the green dot displaying their GPS location. "Whiskey, Quebec, one-seven-niner..."

1115 HRS

1

The tactical analysis feedback facility was a large metal building on main post surrounded by steel gates and high radio antennas. Inside, the crusty old retiree, Kerry Douglas, sat behind a computer and took down the grid Sergeant First Class Delequa reported. Kerry's ensemble was one for the ages. Snakeskin boots and denim fabric from head to toe, accompanied by a cowboy hat. An utter fashion nightmare that would send the queerest of the queer running for the hills with no hope of adjusting. Computers, printers, and supplies cluttered the office.

His cubicle was in a room with no windows, miles away from the box. The building sat conveniently near the commanding general's office, so that any emergencies or changes within the simulation would come from the three-star general himself. This rarely occurred. Only in a state of an emergency or soldier death would the big man grace his presence amongst the facility.

It mainly housed military contractors and civilians, most of them retired and settled in the surrounding area. Soldiers working in the facility were of higher echelons. The civilian's job was to assist the green suitors in accomplishing their tasks by providing them information and updates about the weather, live fire exercises, scheduled detonations in the area, changes to scenario design and locations of opposing forces on the simulated battlefield. Many of these workers have held their positions for years.

2

Kerry's untamed mustache pressed against the radio receiver, writing the grid coordinate number by number.

"All right, let me run it down for ya,"' Kerry said. "Thanks, eight-Charlie."

"No problem."

"Kilo five-eight out," Delequa closed out the transmission.

Kerry leaned back in his leather chair and placed his feet upon the wobbly desk. Large maps displaying the military installation and all its training areas populated the walls surrounding the cubicles filled with retired government contractors.

"Who just called up that grid?" asked Carl, the office section leader. His main responsibility was to collect and track all unit locations moving across the box.

"Our favorite Walker, Sergeant First Class Delequa," Kerry replied.

He ran his fingers through the dirt squirrel growing on his upper lip and spoke loudly for everyone to hear.

"You know what? Fuck that guy! He's an asshole. I ain't running shit down for him."

"Don't do him like that," Stanley said from the neighboring desk, half-laughing and half serious. His bald head shone bright as the sun.

"Now you're being an asshole, Kerry," Carl joked, standing up from behind his desk. His tall black stature intimidated those who didn't know him. "You better get off your ass and run that grid down. While you're at it, stop by your momma's house and change that outfit."

Deep manly chuckles erupted. With that, Kerry stood up and proceeded to make himself fresh coffee. Most of his counterparts paid him no attention while others continued to clown on his denim outfit. The statement Kerry made was brash, but accurate. Delequa was an asshole.

After pouring the coffee, Kerry returned to his desk, plotted the grid on a gigantic map against the wall behind his desk and made a phone call to range control. Once the conversation ended, he picked up the microphone.

1118 HRS

1

"Sergeant First Class Delequa, this is Mr. Kerry, come in, over."

"Go for Delequa, send it."

"Congratulations," Kerry joked, "you're not in an impact zone, and no other units are reportedly in your vicinity."

"Thank you, Mr. Kerry," Delequa said, "I appreciate it."

"Call if you need anything else, out."

Delequa walked back towards the soldiers, stepping quietly over shrubbery. He walked heel to toe, a technique taught to soldiers in the old days. A block of instruction Delequa never erased from his memory.

"Listen up. My civilian counterparts on main post checked to see if anyone's out here," Delequa informed, sliding another dip in his mouth. "No one is reported out this way."

Mechanical rumblings rang out a tale of mystery, further arousing the group's curiosity.

"Did a vehicle just start up?"

"That's what it sounded like," Hines said, "probably another unit out here."

"That startup was too quiet for a tactical vehicle," Delequa advised.

"Well, let's find out," Hines suggested. "Better than sitting here finger blasting our buttholes."

"But I'm tired, Sergeant, we need to get on our way," Calhoun confessed.

"Shut the fuck up, Calhoun," Hines fired back, half serious. "You only live once."

"Yolo," Calhoun whined.

The team took several steps and stopped. Light conversation bounced from branch to branch, drifting on the summer wind.

"I said shut the fuck up!"

Hines cast concern to Delequa; both soldiers developed an interest in the vocalization. Calhoun stood fixed, holding his useless rifle at the low ready, privately wanting the day to be over. All he wanted was to lie down and sleep. At times like this, he considered returning to the streets, go back to gangbanging again. It was less physical stress on his body, and it didn't take a five-paragraph operations order to rob a liquor store. But his prideful side would never let him go back to that life.

2

"Well," Delequa huffed, "looks like we're headed for it anyways. Might as well find out who's fucking around in the sticks."

He felt something was off. Unease overcame Delequa's stomach. A feeling he knew came each time he tempted fate.

It was the most ignored human instinct, and the most accurate impulse to follow.

"I hope it's G-Man," Calhoun wished. "I'm tired of all this walking. I'm ready for a fight."

"Careful what you wish for," Delequa moralized.

Staff Sergeant Hines performed a sensitive item inventory check on Calhoun, patting down his weapon and visually laying eyes on the FM radio tucked away in the rucksack.

"Fuck it, we'll leave our rucks, kit and helmets here. We come back and grab them after we figure out what we're dealing with. Just bring your weapon in case it is G-man. We don't want them circling around and taking our weapons. We'll face UCMJ action if those sensitive items get taken." Hines briefed.

"Roger that," Calhoun agreed, "I've had enough of this damn rucksack."

Calhoun let the pack free fall from his shoulder blades and crash atop a massive fern. Hines did the same. Both soldiers took swigs of water and stretched their upper extremities, then secured their weapons.

"Ready," Hines murmured.

"Roger that, Sergeant."

"After y'all," Delequa insisted, motioning his arm forward like a welcoming butler. Shifting into a single file line with Hines leading the way, Delequa followed in the rear, worried. They wove around ferns and bushes, slowly ascending. Before reaching the top of the hill, the woman's voice came again.

"Denis! Denis! Wake up!"

Seconds later, a song Shelton Hines hadn't heard since high school resonated through the trees.

1120 HRS

1

In the depths of the Louisiana forest, Hines flight-or-fight response triggered. Police Officers, Firefighters, and emergency responders all relate to the phenomenon. It is a heightened sense in times of dangerous circumstances.

"Get down," Hines motioned.

"Stop it! Stop it!"

The men dropped to the prone, hearts racing faster than the rising humidity and sweltering heat, both focused on the point man.

2

Ahead of the surveying group lay a clearing in the woods in which there was a three-member party. Tied to a tree was a nude woman, whimpering and crying. Directly across from her was a nude man, also tied to a tree and enduring a strenuous masturbation from a third character, comically dressed as a bearded lumberjack. The bound parties were at the mercy of his violence. In the middle of the gap, a red truck ran idle blaring the music.

The image of the violent sexual assault pierced Hines's mind, carving forever into his brain. He looked back to his young troop and motioned him closer. Calhoun materialized to the left of his teammate. The sight was unlike anything Calhoun had ever seen, even on the mean streets of Baton Rouge.

"What's going on up there?" Delequa fussed.

With a forceful display for silence, Hines slammed his index finger to his lips—the universal hand gesture for shut the fuck up—and then rolled back to his belly to observe. Hating he was uniformed, and slightly aggravated and confused, Delequa low crawled up the hill to the team, dodging a fire ant hill along the way. Breathing heavily, he arrived at the right of Hines and dug his elbows deep into the hard ground.

"Give me a SITREP," Delequa demanded.

Hines considered the acronym used to provide situational reports to leaders requesting it, which consisted of the three D's: distance, direction, and description. "Hundred meters, twelve o'clock, a guy has two people bound to trees, both naked," Hines reported, "and he's..."

"Stop it now! What's wrong with you?!"

His concentration broken, Hines's update trailed off as he stared through the thin greenery toward the screams. The lumberjack, dressed oddly in long-sleeved flannel, jerked the naked man's cock with an escalating violence.

"He's what?" Delequa requested.

Hines snapped out of his stupor, throat dry and cracking, "Jerking the guy off."

Delequa was unable to respond to the crazy feedback and scooted up further to see for himself. His eyes widened as he eyed the lumberjack issue the unwanted hand job to a semi-conscious man.

"Scream you wife fuckin' piece of shit! Scream, boy!"

Calhoun, speechless and disturbed, wanted to look away, but couldn't. It was like watching a train wreck. The funky pop of the snare drum and grungy guitars painted the soundtrack of sexual assault and murder.

"What do we do?" Calhoun finally asked.

"We hold tight," Delequa suggested. "Let me radio back our grid and see if they can send someone out."

"This far in the bush?"

"It's a fucking start, Sergeant," Delequa bitched, "you got a better suggestion?"

Hines's hero complex ignited. "We must do something. Can't just sit on our asses and watch these people die."

"It's not our responsibility."

"It is our fucking responsibility, Big Sarge." Hines urged. "We swore an oath to protect the citizens of this country against all enemies, both foreign and domestic."

3

Despite the medals awarded to Staff Sergeant Hines for bravery and courage, Delequa was far more battle tested and seasoned. A true killer, ruthless when called for, a monster born of failure and guilt. Hines had the better career on paper, the shiny gold and silver medals displayed on his chest for everyone to see in his dress blues, but after Jason Robertson's death, William Delequa racked five confirmed kills, more than any soldier in his battalion, and he never missed a night's sleep over it. His actions earned him a reputation, known for praising violence of action, creating meat-eating leaders within his ranks, and popping a round in anyone's chest if the situation called for it without blinking an eye. Jason's death haunted him, not the sunburnt faces of dead cowards and religious extremists. And he knew better than to judge a man on distinguished awards.

As his mentors had instilled, "Know their character and stature; examine it if you must."

4

"I don't give a fuck about that bullshit," Delequa growled, "no one is trying to be a hero today. That nut job could have weapons up there. What are we gonna do, fire blanks in his general direction, maybe land a butt stroke on his crazy ass if we get close enough?"

"It doesn't matter what he has up there. If we move quickly, we can take him down," Calhoun insisted. "All I've seen is a knife."

"Shut the fuck up, Private," Delequa grunted.

"Don't speak to my soldier like that, Sergeant First Class."

"Or what, motherfucker?" Delequa threatened, his eyes wide and crazed. "Whatcha gonna do, prick? Bring an empty gun to a knife fight?"

Showing no fear, Hines moved his body over until it rubbed against Delequa's. "I refuse to sit here like a coward."

"Being smart is not the same as being a coward, dumbass." Delequa held his stare.

"Insult me one more fucking time, Big Sarge, and I'll put rank aside and ball your ass up in these woods," Hines warned.

Before Delequa could respond to the challenge, the ongoing savagery increased, sending the naked

man screaming for all to hear.

"Oh my God! Oh God, no!"

5

Mr. Lumberjack was now hacking off the naked man's penis with the knife. The team collectively felt sick, their lunches were seconds from coming back up the pipe. Calhoun placed his forehead on the ground and prayed, something he hadn't done since week three of basic training. Hines stared down in disgust, a relentless heroism brewing in his veins, growing harder to hold back. Delequa coldly watched the dismemberment unfold, never turning his hardened eyes.

"Look Honey, he's a squirter just like you!"

The lumberjack raised the naked man's member over his head. He looked like the Predator proclaiming victory with his skull and spine trophies. The woman continued to beg her God and the wilderness for help.

"Please, somebody help us! Please!"

Without saying a word, Delequa disengaged from the event and shimmied down the hill, ready to notify higher command. A growing urgency stopped him halfway down the incline as he debated calling his son instead of the task force commander. For the first time, as a leader in the Army, he didn't know what to do. He pulled out his cellphone. Fear was overcoming his decision making, and he didn't understand why. As a soldier he'd been in far worse situations than this and survived, reactions were typically automatic. Their biggest issue was not having live rounds for their weapons. If Delequa had just one bullet, this psychotic mess would be over, along with the Lumberjack's life. In his soul, something was wrong.

Delequa mishandled the phone, and it slid down the hillside like a hockey puck on ice.

"Shit," Delequa pursued it.

6

Before reclassifying to a Cavalry scout in 2010, Delequa began his career as a Military Police Officer. Then, months before leaving on his second deployment to Afghanistan, Delequa achieved the rank of Sergeant. He was young and inexperienced like most and transitioning from follower to leader had been the toughest transformation he had in the military. One day he was on the same playing field as his battle buddies, then BOOM, he was leading them into combat, responsible for their mental and physical health, and by extension, that of their families.

He also wore the stress of his personal relationship with his son on his face, which at one point, led to a female soldier in his platoon taking interest in him. She wanted to help fill the gap of unhappiness in his life with her soft breasts and tight pussy. He knew better than to shit where he slept. It was like the golden rule; everywhere, with all employees, and especially the Army. But that rule didn't apply to Delequa. Pussy was pussy, and he'd get it where he could.

This mistaken line of thinking had borne him a child before and apparently taught him nothing. He loved the feeling of being in an unauthorized relationship. Deep down, Delequa knew that his fun-loving personality made him a platoon favorite, and sometimes the military protected favorites. In this case, that was true. Leaders knew about the couple. A young Sergeant banging a Specialist wasn't a new concept, and Army regulations demanded they act, but his leaders only reprimanded him at the lowest of levels.

Breaking the good order and discipline of the platoon was detrimental to the mission, but there was no good headway in Afghanistan, nor would there ever be. No doubt Delequa was flawed, imperfect like the rest of humanity. He loved the pleasure of being between his comrade's thighs, but also cherished his other platoon mates. The fear of not making it back home brought them all together. They lived day by day, sometimes carelessly and dangerously, never knowing what the desert would bring to them once they left the comfort of Kandahar Airbase.

The bell tolled one scorching summer day, in a place the desert burned hotter than the deepest level of hell. The Taliban were still relevant in the fight, and ISIS was but a mere twinkle in a goat fucker's eye. The platoon's convoy of military vehicles stopped on the outskirts of Kandahar city, a cesspool of filth and disease, to pull security and establish a hasty checkpoint from which they could search for the smuggling of illegal weapons and explosives into the city.

Inside the city, the streets flooded with sewage, emitting a putrid aroma that traveled several kilometers in all directions, yet it continued to draw vendors, merchants, and butchers to its street corners, each hoping to make a sale. A single US dollar went a long way for the local Afghan worker. It wasn't a shock to see the selling of bootleg DVDs, cartons of cigarettes, high-quality mink blankets, and exotic animals. The entire country was nefarious and lacked color. The human eye became accustomed to brown, tan, and light green, and when a bright pigment hit the eye, it was sensory overload. The brain reacted as if it was seeing a Disney film for the first time. If a passing convoy commander had the gall, they would stop and purchase several items from a seller. If you knew no better, it looked like a drug deal going down next to a police station. Quickly, the service members hopped back into their vehicle and sped back to base.

When patrolling through Kandahar City, speed was your safety. It is harder to hit a fast-moving target than a slow one, and truth be told, the Taliban were horrible shots, missing more often than Stormtroopers. Even more, reports throughout the theater of operations were that the Kandahar city Police Chief was corrupt to the bone and had ties to the Taliban. If the police chief was smuggling weapons inside the city to reinforce Taliban fighters and help carry out attacks on military personnel entering the city, Delequa's squad would find out.

The squad consisted of three up-armored HUMVEEs with nine soldiers in tow equipped with full combat loads, machine guns and rifles. Salt from the sweat caused by the heavy body armor glued to their torsos stained their desert combat uniforms. Most of them were not a day over twenty-five years old, young men and women sent to fight old men's wars. The squad positioned their vehicles tactically and soldiers swiftly dismounted, except for the Gunners who pulled security behind mounted fifty-caliber machine guns.

The soldiers deployed concertina wire across the heavily damaged asphalt of the Afghanistan highway. Orange traffic cones greeted travelers from Pakistan in the south and lead the way through the checkpoint north into Kandahar city. Once completing the setup, the soldiers took up positions that provided security for one another. The squad leader remained in the middle of the checkpoint for command and control, issuing orders to subordinates that searched every fifth vehicle entering the area.

For hours under the deathly sun, the squad remained vigilant in their duty, guzzling water to ensure they didn't become heat causalities. No one wanted to die that way, and there was no faster way to be labeled a poontang than collapsing due to heat exhaustion. The ridicule would be hard as fuck, and it was unlikely you'd live it down. Squad members gulped all they could, making intermittent runs to the back hatch of their vehicles to refill their camelbacks from tan colored five-gallon water jugs.

Ahead of the checkpoint, a bit further south of the city, local Afghan police teams smoked opium next to their rundown patrol cars that had no backseats or windows. They threw debris at passing cars as they entered the city. Cops partaking in drug abuse was routine practice with the police of Kandahar. Raping and pillaging small villages for profit and pleasure was next on their list. This was common practice. Delequa had witnessed Afghan men rape and molest underaged boys, passing them around villages and campfires for a good dicking, then go home to fuck their enslaved wives. As the saying went, 'Women were for procreation, boys were for pleasure.' Soldiers on tour in the country quickly learned about it, witnessed it all firsthand, but were expected to ignore and forget about it. On multiple occasions, locals had offered

Delequa and his squad sex with young boys in exchange for pairs of Wiley X sunglasses. That was the truth that never made it to television. It was sickening. In Delequa's opinion, the culture deserved to die. He often laughed at the bashing of American police officers. He had seen firsthand the terror of living in a truly oppressive regime. Outside the wire, nothing was off the table.

On the border of the checkpoint, groups of teenagers would form moving in close, to beg for food and water. The vagabonds often moved in clusters larger than any zombie herd on *The Walking Dead*, and if not controlled, they could overrun a position. This increased the danger of attack from suicide vests, which children disguised by the crowd often wore. Soldiers would die a quick death if detonated, all because of a kind heart.

Delequa didn't believe in winning hearts and minds. That only got soldiers killed. That day, the importance had not been the wants and needs of the local populace, but the safety of the soldiers.

7

After five hours in the desert heat, Delequa's lover and teammate, Melissa Jensen, needed to relieve herself. Delequa lay in the prone position providing security with his M4 carbine rifle atop a natural berm over watching the southeast end of the checkpoint area. Melissa tossed a rock and struck Delequa's helmet, rattling his dome. A quick surge of panic rushed through Delequa's veins as he looked over his right shoulder to the southwest, from which the object came. Melissa motioned him over with a flick of the neck, and quickly his nerves calmed. Both stood up from their positions and the fifty-cal gunner in the HUMVEE's turret, Jason Robertson, shook his head disapprovingly. He never supported the relationship, especially being close with Delequa on a personal level outside of work and knowing his past and the deep regrets there. Robertson had values, much like Delequa's parents had tried to instill in him.

Robertson called up for approval via his FM radio, and moments later, he signaled to his teammates they were good to go relieve themselves. The two lovebirds made their way across the uneven desert en route to an abandoned shanty. Once they arrived, they conducted a typical search of the building at the high ready, weapons drawn into their shoulders. A wooden gate led the soldiers into a small, empty courtyard with assorted prayer rugs and teapots. Afghans loved chi more than a hipster loved Starbucks. Delequa cleared the cramped, lone room of the compound and entered back into the courtyard where he found his sweetheart propped against the wall, pissing like a racehorse. The bright yellow liquid struck the sand parting it like Moses separating the red sea. Delequa walked over, and before she could wipe her crotch with a baby wipe, he threw himself onto her fondling her clitoris. His appetite for love was sometimes filthy and uncontrollable. They kissed passionately, as he rubbed her lady parts with a circular motion, his hard cock pressed against her, pulsating with desire. Delequa inserted two fingers into her vagina and instantly sounds of bliss ensued. He removed his Kevlar and jammed his head into the side of her neck and sucked, all the while finger fucking her in hopes of climax.

As she moaned, producing ever more vaginal secretions, a loud blast from the operating grounds disrupted their love shack moment. Followed by a massive explosion, forceful enough to shake the wall the pair shared. Expeditiously, Delequa snapped back to reality, retracting his fingers, and gathering his equipment before exiting the courtyard. Melissa remained against the mud-hardened wall, struggling with her pants still below her knees.

Delequa stumbled onward to a scene he'd never be able to forget. The HUMVEE that transported the team to their current destination was ablaze, burning red hot, scorching everything within feet, including his teammate, Jason Robertson, whose screams were louder than the gunfire at the northern edge of the checkpoint. The squad had come under attack from three Taliban fighters, all shrouded in black robes, masks that hid their cowardly faces, and wearing Nike running shoes. The only piece of the ensemble that was worth a fuck was the shoes, helping them to glide across the sharp rocks with ease and speed. They had successfully eliminated the fifty-cal on the HUMVEE with a rocket-propelled grenade shot from the periphery of Kandahar City.

Without hesitation or concern of safety, Delequa sprinted towards the engulfed vehicle. His friend's screams were heart wrenching and full of torment. As he neared, bullets buzzed overhead. Sheer chaos unfolded, as soldiers yelled commands and adjusted fighting positions to prepare against the advancing enemy, returning fire when necessary. Still, Delequa's focus was on saving Jason. Once he reached the vehicle, the conflagration was impenetrable and allowed no hope for rescue. There would be no attempt to retrieve his fellow soldier; the flames singed his combat uniform as he stood and watched the truck burn, forever implanting a sense of regret and shame to his heart. He watched the flesh peel away from Jason's face as hellfire consumed him.

When the encounter was over, Specialist Jason Robertson and three Taliban fighters had lost their lives. Robertson would be the only casualty from the platoon during the yearlong deployment. Several days following the attack, the entire base attended Jason's memorial service at Kandahar Airbase. Afterward, William Delequa ended the illicit relationship. He would never be the same, mentally, or spiritually.

1126 HRS

1

On the hilltop where the Cockaded Woodpecker had fled, the two-man team watched as the madman continued to commit crimes. Both men, ill with antipathy, did nothing more than watch the lawlessness. The chaos ate Hines alive. He wiggled and shifted impatiently in the earth, biting his bottom lip until it drew blood. The situation petrified Calhoun; his mind lost in consternation. The day he raised his right hand to swear life to God and country, he never thought he'd find himself in this predicament stateside. A morning of hot bloodshed and massacre. Before their eyes, tragedy unfolded on a citizen they'd sworn to protect as another became the enemy. And with the clock racing against them, all hope seemed lost. Blank ammunition filled the rifles carried by the team, providing no help outside the training exercise.

"If I had live rounds," Hines divulged, "I'd put a bullet in him."

Calhoun looked to his leader with expanded, alarmed eyes. "What are we gonna do, Sergeant?"

"I don't know."

"You hurt me! And ya' destroyed my marriage! I'll never have a family now!"

The team watched the lunatic lecture, bellowing his woes to the world and the all heavenly father.

"Jesus Christ," Hines panted, "this guy's fucking insane."

"I didn't sign up for this." Calhoun moaned.

Hines was taken aback by the soldier's statement but waited a moment before responding. "Like hell you didn't," Hines snarled, teeth clenched together, "this is exactly what you signed up for." He reached over to grasp Calhoun's collar. "this makes us different. We are the one per-centers of the world, citizens that have taken the oath to protect all we love, even if that love isn't returned. We are soldiers. Men and women ordered to do the devil's work when the time comes, because the rest of the world is too pussy to do it themselves. This world is filled with snowflakes and cowards." Hines released the soldier's collar and banged his fist into his chest, passionately. "I'm no coward, and I damn sure have no pity for one. If you're gonna sit here and tremble before the enemy, then you're no soldier of mine, and you haven't realized the hazard of your chosen profession. I've taken my obligation seriously, Private Calhoun, maybe you're a coward just like the rest."

"By God, Kurt, please, don't! You can't do this! I'm your wife!"

Calhoun listened like a scolded child, the harsh words penetrating his pride, but they were true. He'd always respected Hines, trusted him with his life, and wouldn't disrespect him, not now. Respect is a two-way street, and tough love isn't easy to swallow.

"This isn't Iraq, Sergeant," Calhoun stressed. "Maybe Big Sarge is right and that psycho isn't our enemy."

"Well, he is today, and we're gonna take the fucker out," Hines fired back.

1128 HRS

1

Down below, on the slope, Delequa brought the mic to his lips.

"Mr. Kerry, this is Sergeant First Class Delequa, come in over."

Nothing.

"I ain't got time for proper radio etiquette, someone answer the fucking radio up there!"

Fuzz emitted from the amplifier, and Mr. Denim Dan finally chimed in.

"Now, now, that's not the way a senior non-commissioned officer is supposed to talk on the radio, over," Kerry picked up.

Delequa leaned back, staring into the clouds, beads of sweat streaming from his rounded cheeks.

"I don't have time to fuck around with you. There's a man out here," Delequa stopped mid- sentence, staring at the mic with bewilderment. The transmission did not deliver. The battery was dead. Frantically, he searched all the pockets in his FLC, including his trouser pockets before realizing he had no replacement. The small, black, metal hydride batteries were collecting dust inside the parked military vehicle, safe in the assembly area.

"Goddamn it," Delequa vocalized.

2

Once more, Delequa pulled out his phone and pressed firmly against the fingerprint reader at the bottom of the cellphone. The device came to life, and to William's bewilderment, the service bar showed no sign of service at all. That sent a wave of panic through his mind. The universe was colluding against them. It was his fault for forgetting the batteries, but never had Delequa had complete dead cell phone coverage during his time as a Walker, thus he rarely carried extra radio batteries. Then again, he'd never traversed this far in the woods by foot, specifically into this part of the training area. Dead spots ran amok over the box, and if you didn't have AT&T, service wasn't guaranteed in the simulated war-zone. But now, in his time of crisis, everything in creation had turned against them.

"Liar!"

Delequa opened the contacts app and scrolled down until he found James's name in big, black bold letters. The fact he couldn't call or message his son killed him. The day had gone to hell in a hand basket, and he wanted more than ever to reach out. Delequa slammed the phone onto the ground, cursing under his breath. No one was coming. Time was of the essence. Two complete strangers needed saving. Delequa did not want to be a savior. Today was not the day to be a hero.

"Help me! Someone! Anyone! Help me!"

The woman's pleas pierced Delequa's ears, forcing his eyes to close. "Think, William, think goddamn it," Delequa sounded like a lunatic to himself. "What the actual fuck? No service, communications are down. Jesus Christ." Fear and frustration ran roughshod over Delequa's warrior spirit, crushing his hardened persona, leaving a frightened civilian. Heavy breaths broke from his sealed lips.

Several feet away in the grass, the serpent returned. The viper's black eyes were soulless, its nostrils wide, the heat sensing pit organs on the side of its head wide open. It was beautiful in color, with light and dark browns blending wonderfully into the environment. It's cold skin grazed Delequa's hand. Instantly, he opened his eyes, snatched the serpent with lightning speed and flung it down the hill. It slid across the earth, coming to rest at the feet of Jason Robertson.

3

William Delequa locked eyes with the ghost from his past, and it terrified him. Jason stood smoldering. Light grey puffs of smoke floated upward from a face deprived of life. Blackened, writhing maggots filled Jason's exposed eye sockets. Delequa gawked at the monster he created.

"Remember who you are," Jason uttered, his skeletal structure motionless, the maggots free-falling to their fate.

"This can't be real," Delequa rationalized.

"Hold onto faith," Jason said walking forward, no sound resonating from his steps. "Understand what must be done."

The specter levitated several feet off the ground as the smell of smoldering death permeated the air.

"Rise above the fear, William." The snake coiled under the floating entity. "Even the fallen one cannot claim you today," Jason grunted, pointing a finger to the serpent.

The voice was haunting. It left Delequa speechless and afraid. He watched the viper transcend into the air, floating upwards. The serpent thrashed in the air till it found purchase and slithered around Jason's leg. The copperhead moved up Jason's body and coiled around his neck, peering down upon Delequa.

Jason floated forward with the wind, slowly gliding until he was directly above Delequa. "What are you prepared to do, William?" Jason challenged.

"Denis! Denis!"

In the blink of an eye, Jason was gone, vanishing between heated rays of summer light. The music from the truck stopped playing right after Jason vanished. The energy in the air was tangible. The atmosphere turned quiet. Unnerved, Delequa rotated onto his belly, low crawling back up to the soldiers with haste. He arrived next to Hines, still unsure if he was crazy.

1132 HRS

1

"Be silent," Hines hissed, "The music stopped a few minutes ago. Keep your voices low, he might hear us." Hines hushed.

"But at least he can't see us," Delequa pointed out.

"Let's hope it stays that way." Calhoun breathed.

"Where'd you go?" Hines asked, confused and angry.

"The lumberjack's stabbing the shit outta him. He's fucking killing him!"

Delequa, unsurprised by the news, noticed Calhoun crying distressed tears.

"I can't watch anymore," Calhoun confessed. Neither leader acknowledged him.

"We gotta do something, Sarge," Hines said, his face concerned, yet determined.

The sound of rending flesh surrounded the soldiers.

"Like what?" Delequa countered. "You wanna take the fight to this guy unarmed?"

"Yes!" Hines answered, without thinking. His voice was passionate but muted.

"We don't know if he has any weapons in that truck. We need to plot the grid and head back to the assembly area."

"Are you fucking serious? You wanna up and leave?"

"Yes."

"What the fuck," Hines lectured, "Didn't you call it up on your radio? Those things work for miles."

"No," Delequa admitted, "my battery's dead."

"What! You didn't bring extras batteries?"

"No goddamn it," Delequa growled, "I accidentally left them in my truck."

"What about your cell?"

"Don't have service."

Hines pounded a fist into the dirt, splitting his knuckles open. "You gotta be fucking shitting me," Hines fretted, "fucking great! If you can't relay back what's going on, that means nobody's coming to help."

"Quiet," Delequa muttered, "Have Calhoun go back down and try his radio again. It might work this time." Delequa suggested.

Calhoun lifted his head from the ground, eyes glossed with sickness, and spoke.

"It won't work, Big Sarge, and you know it. Everything's gone wrong. Sergeant Hines is right," Calhoun swallowed the terror in his throat, "We have to do something."

"No one asked for your input, Private," Delequa interjected. "I'm the senior non-commissioned officer here, and we're heading back."

"It'll be too late then," Calhoun responded.

"I don't give a shit," Delequa huffed.

Abruptly, Hines grabbed Delequa by the fatigues and pulled him close.

"Who the fuck do you think you are?" Hines challenged. "You're not acting like a Sergeant First Class in the United

States Army! That woman needs our help, and we're gonna help her."

"Get your fucking hands off me, Sergeant," Delequa silently demanded, returning the embrace and grasping Hines by the filthy collar of his sweat-soaked uniform. "You don't know who you're talking to."

"Oh, I know exactly who I'm talking to," Hines said through gritted teeth, "you're a fucking coward, and a pitiful excuse for a leader."

Delequa placed his sweaty, skinny nose against the disrespectful soldier's snout.

"Keep disrespecting me and I'll end you, motherfucker," Delequa threatened. "I'll take the matter higher."

"I'm not your enemy, Big Sarge," Hines strained, releasing Delequa's combat uniform. He pointed forward, "that lunatic out there is."

"This isn't our fight," Delequa passionately proclaimed.

"The flag we wear on this uniform represents hope, freedom, and salvation, especially to those in need," Hines continued.

"I don't care what it represents, no one's playing the hero today, Sergeant," Delequa whispered. "I will not allow your team to take action."

Defeat crept across Hines's face as he realized Delequa lacked the courage to do the right thing. His voice faded to a mere whisper. "You've lost the warrior spirit. You've betrayed your oath. You think a helpless woman's life is less than yours."

"That's not the case," Delequa snapped. "Your lives are worth more. Soldiers' lives are worth more. No one's dying on my watch."

Hines understood the logic of the angry, salty soldier. His general concern for troops was still a priority. A man easy to work for, but not with.

"Fuck this," Calhoun cursed, rolling to his side and yanking a rock from the earth.

"What the fuck are you doing?" Delequa close-mouthed, releasing Hines's uniform and sliding over the Californian.

In a flash, Calhoun rose to his knees, and threw the rock towards the psychopath before Delequa could reach him. Delequa put Calhoun on the ground and mounted him like a UFC fighter.

The rock easily missed the target, landing near the crazed Lumberjack. Delequa placed a dirty hand over Calhoun's mouth.

"Don't make a sound," Delequa sighed.

Hines buried his face in the dirt, motionless. Delequa lay atop Calhoun, whose black face was now a lighter shade than it had been moments before. Delequa looked forward through the dense brush. The lumberjack was looking in their direction.

"Does he see us?" Hines murmured, mud and soil caking his lips.

"Nobody breathe," Delequa muttered.

"Who's there?"

Delequa stared into the wide, scared eyes of Calhoun. The kid didn't blink, or breathe, as perspiration beaded and rolled from his forehead down the side of his smooth, black face. Delequa issued a small, reassuring nod and mouthed, "Stay calm."

"Come out you fuckin' coward! I know someone's there!"

The angered and controlled debate between the two leaders had not yet exposed them, but their luck was running out. Delequa tried to understand Calhoun's action. It was irresponsible, a poor decision that should have completely exposed them to a deranged killer. What was the logic of throwing a rock? A fucking rock! Calhoun was no David and the Lumberjack sure as shit wasn't Goliath.

A warmth of emotions hit Delequa suddenly, mentally checking him out. Moments of his life begin to flash before his eyes. Snippets of once treasured memories, forgotten through years of perpetual anger.

2

Having received an **A** in math on his report card, Delequa's smiling and proud mother planted a kiss on his lips. A smooch so powerful he repeatedly recalled it later in life. Outside of the occasional phone call, she hadn't been in his life for years, and her absence had furtively eaten away at him.

The vision flashed forward to the embrace of his two best friends from high school moments before he stepped into the bus that carried him to Basic Training. Good friends he had known his entire life. Played ball with, discovered girls with. The friends that helped him through his first heartbreak. Friends he cruised the streets with for years, raising hell, not a care in the world. Friends that knew all the girls he slept with on the dance and flag teams. Friends he hadn't seen or heard from in twenty years.

The most powerful memory hit like a freight train. Delequa hugged his son for the first time, a meaningful moment captured in time. The scent of coconut invaded his senses. That day, his son's hair smelled like a beach in Hawaii, emitting a strong tropical scent.

Then a thick darkness moved through his subconscious. From the blackness, Jason emerged, drifting across the gloom. He was exactly how Delequa remembered him. Not charred to the bone or rotting, no poisonous serpent. Just Jason, youthfulness restored, shining brightly in the obscurity.

"Remember who you are," Jason said, his face sincere and full of life. "Let go of the bitterness and regret you carry. It is eating away like a cancer. I will protect you from the dark one, William," Jason began to fade.

"Don't forget, to the world we are nothing..." and with that, he vanished.

3

"But to each other... we are everything." Delequa repeated.

"Please! Help me!"

"What," Hines looked to Calhoun with concern. Calhoun remained silent, his eyes wider than the mouth of the Mississippi.

"Please, I know someone's out there! I can feel it! Please! Help me!"

"I warned you, woman!"

"To the world we are nothing, but to each other," Delequa paused, sadness forming around his eyes, "We are everything."

Delequa's old platoon sergeant in Afghanistan used the phrase daily. It was a way to motivate the troops, empowering them to carry out any mission on the docket. Every time they went out on patrol, the squads would proclaim the mantra to each another. There was much meaning and emotion behind the quote.

Delequa had spoken the truism directly to Jason the day he died. A betrayed oath. He hadn't uttered it again, until now.

4

"Help! Please, I know someone's out there!"

Delequa looked to Hines with sorrowful inspiration. "You're right," Delequa confessed. "No one else needs to die today." His low voice emitted conviction, as his demeanor shifted. "Now...what are we prepared to do?"

As if he'd been waiting on the declaration, a smile spread to the corners of Hines's mouth.

"Welcome back, Big Sarge! No more hiding. We were born and bred for this. It's time to roll out."

"Goddamn right it is," Delequa's aggression seethed.

"Stay away!"

In unison, the group looked up to see the lumberjack kneeling in front of the woman's crotch. Delequa maneuvered from Calhoun and watched in disgust.

"No! Get away from me!"

Through the bushes, the crew of soldiers saw an orange flame graze across the woman's pubic area. Her screams were deafening. Calhoun covered his ears, feeling her misery.

"By God, he's frying her," Hines gasped.

"I can see that," Delequa growled, "we need to move, ASAP."

"We flank him," Hines announced, breaking eye contact with the foul scene.

"Kill me! Kill me!"

Calhoun pressed against his ears harder. "From which direction?" Delequa asked.

"The right," Hines briefed, visualizing the attack. "Leave our weapons here since they're useless. They'll just slow us down. We can assume he's got more toys in the back of that truck. Need to draw him away. I'll take Calhoun and assault him from that brush." Hines pointed to a thick set of high shrubs to the right of the clearing. "Her screams will cover our movement."

"What do you need me to do?"

"Once we engage, run up the middle and free the hostage. Keep trying the phone while we maneuver."

Delequa acknowledged the plan with a nod.

"How to initiate the attack?" Hines pondered aloud.

Delequa opened the biggest pouch on his FLC and removed one of the two hand grenade simulators within. The device was no larger than a baseball, but cylinder shaped. There was a small metal clip on the top that unlatched, priming the explosive. Beneath it, a thick white string dangled. Warning stickers covered the explosive. The largest one read:

WARNING
EXPLOSIVE MAY CAUSE LOSS OF LIFE,
LIMB, OR EYESIGHT

"Rock him with this bad boy," Delequa said proudly, slamming it into Hines's hand.

"Roger that," Hines smiled.

"Nothing to it but to do it," Delequa rhymed.

Hines squirmed over and removed one of Calhoun's hands from his ear.

"Calhoun," Hines hissed, "follow me."

Delequa grabbed Hines by the forearm. "Be careful. Don't make a sound. Initiate contact with the grenade simulator and take him down quick. I'll be up the middle the moment contact is made." Delequa squeezed tighter. "No hesitations; the whole plan could shit the bed fast. No one else needs to die today."

"Roger, everybody wants to be a hero until it's time to do hero shit," Hines replied, grasping Delequa in the warrior's grip. He cut a quick smile and was off, low crawling to the coordinated position.

"You'll be fine, kid," Delequa reassured, as the young soldier followed, "Stick close to Sergeant Hines, and execute with extreme prejudice."

"Violence solves everything," Calhoun groaned.

"Yes, it does," agreed Delequa.

Calhoun issued a salute, knowing damn well Delequa wasn't a field grade officer.

5

Delequa retrieved his phone from the storage pouch, spilling the last remaining sunflower seeds to the ground. There were still no service bars. The sun above sizzled as Delequa stared at the screen, scrolling through his contacts until he saw his son's name. Tears of regret mixed with perspiration trickled down his face. He knew he might never see or speak to his son again, and it crushed him. Combat is unpredictable and often final. No second chances with the enemy. A soldier's mind always considers worst-case scenario, as it should. That is what their training teaches them, so that no matter the outcome, a course of action is always in mind.

Despite no service, Delequa typed a text to his son.

James I want you to know I love you very much and am sorry for many things but know you make me very proud I love you son always remember that

His fingers trembled as he pressed the blue SEND icon on the device. Quickly, the message replied:

UNABLE TO SEND

6

A heartfelt message lost to a Decepticon of technology. He stuffed the phone back into its pouch. The tears flowed more heavily. A soldier's pride in his military reputation is no small matter. Leaders never allowed troops to see their weaknesses; if cracks are found, they won't follow. Individuals in the military must be machines. Emotionless killers that can switch to autopilot during a fray. Delequa broke down into sobs that shook his entire body. He didn't make a sound, but the pressure inside his chest was heavy, almost unbearable.

A muscle under his eye twitched uncontrollably as dysphoria overtook the veteran. Fear would not control him, but it could fuel his rage. The tears turned to anger, the anger into determination. His warrior spirit had regained control. Fear had used the guilt in his heart to win for such a long time, but today he would bury it in battle. Where actions were forever etched in stone, and nothing was ever certain.

Ahead, a chainsaw revved into existence.

7

Delequa's fingers sunk into the dirt, peeling back layers of earth. A mother-fucking chainsaw entered the mix, and the Lumberjack was going to town. Things were getting shittier than a German scat film. Delequa refused to watch the dismemberment. His heart pounded against the bones in his chest.

"Die, soldier boy!"

He could hear the saw consuming flesh and bone.

Part four:
THE DEPARTURE

1140 HRS
15 August 2017

1

Mr. Kerry paused his YouTube video as the radio crackled to life in the Tactical Analysis Feedback Facility.

"Any station to this net, this is Voodoo Seven, come in over," the voice was in panic.

Perturbed, he leaned forward, stroking his bushy mustache and answered the transmission.

"Voodoo seven, you're on Task Force five's net, who are you trying to reach, over?"

"I'm trying to get ahold of anyone," the walker announced. "I've been lost with an infantry squad for a few hours now. I believe we're near Khushal, break," the soldier paused. "I think someone's in trouble out here. Sounds like people are being killed, over."

Kerry felt his heart hit the floor, as his old soldier instincts kicked in. A disposition he hadn't felt since Vietnam. He immediately recalled Delequa's last transmission.

Kerry looks over to the cubicle across from him. "Stan," he called out.

Stan heard Kerry, but he ignored him. The old bastard was a constant joker.

"Stanley, I know you can hear me, you bald-ass bitch!" Kerry taunted.

Stanley Bonner, a retired Army commo-specialist and hardcore gambler, turned his chair to face Kerry.

"What do you want, Kerry?"

"Remember that last transmission with Delequa?"

"Yeah, you checked the grid for him, right?"

"Yeah," Kerry said pausing, "did he sound like he was in any kind of trouble to you?"

"How the fuck am I supposed to know, Kerry," Stan griped, "anything else I can help you with?"

"Yeah, tell your sister to stop stealing my goddamn horses and selling 'em to the Mexicans," Kerry clapped back. The entire office exploded with laughs.

"Y'all shut the fuck up," Kerry said, standing up from his desk. "Since I've got everyone's goddamn attention, I think we got an issue."

"What kinda issue you talking about, Kerry?" Carl asked as everyone piped down.

The veteran's eyes widened as a lump of nerves slid down his throat. "I think we got a big fucking issue, Carl."

2

"*Ava*!"

Staff Sergeant Hines reached the destination and was ready for action. He had concocted the final plan of attack as best he could.

"I'm faster than you, Calhoun, so I need you to initiate the attack. Pop the clip, pull the string, and get this goddamn simulator as close to the lumberjack as possible. Got it?"

Calhoun didn't debate and took the simulator. "Got it, Sergeant."

"Once you throw, I'm taking off heels to ass. The detonation will stun him, Big Sarge will head up the middle to rescue the girl, and you play catch up. I'll have hands on the lumberjack by the time you arrive."

"So, basically execute a modified Battle Drill 1A, correct, Sergeant?"

"Roger, that," Hines huffed.

"I'll catch up, Sergeant," Calhoun promised. "Trust me."

Hines squeezed the back of Calhoun's neck and nodded. He took a deep breath and assumed a three-point stance.

"Now!" Hines low-pitched.

Immediately, Private First-Class Calhoun came to a knee, popped the pin, and pulled the string. The device hissed like a satanic serpent as the ex-gangbanger fired it. Staff Sergeant Hines rose from the foliage, sprinting across the terrain at breakneck speed. His heart beat with courage and confidence; today he would be the hero.

Hines ran hard, much like his days on the football field. He leapt over a small log without breaking stride, his athleticism on full display. The simulator flew high in the air, descending a few yards behind the cock collecting Leatherface of Louisiana. A beautiful placement throw, one that would've earned Private Calhoun the Army's grenade qualification bar. Hines ran with everything he had.

Calhoun moved forward, eyes focused on the simulator's prior flight path. Focused to a fault, he tripped on the log his leader had cleared just moments ago. Calhoun crashed to the ground like a track and field star failing to clear a hurdle. Upon impact, his front teeth penetrated his lower lip, chipping several on the hard ground. Dazed, he put his hand to face, feeling the broken teeth and blood oozing from the puncture. Blood sprayed from his mouth as he got back to his feet, lumbering to catch up with his fearless leader.

Hines's adrenaline took over. He visualized the explosion, the target's disorientation, and a thunderous tackle to save the day.

"Drop it, fuckface," Hines screeched.

3

Kurt heard the attacker's approach and stopped mere feet from his final victim. The jig was up. Nothing ever goes according to plan. If it did, there'd be far more unsolved murders in the world. In his half-drunken mind, the fact someone had been present in the woods all along was unbelievable. Truly, out of all the spots in the forest, someone had to pop out of the sticks to play hero and rain on his parade. Well, not today, cocksucker. Kurt dug his left foot into the dirt and relaxed his hips, ready to pivot. He didn't want to acknowledge the charging voyeur too soon. Black smoke rolled from the exhaust as he revved the chainsaw.

4

Delequa lay flat on his belly. The single grenade simulator left in his FLC pouch made the position uncomfortable.

"Take him down, boys," Delequa said, "Close the distance and finish it." He closed his eyes, breathing calmly, awaiting the explosion.

"He won't make it," Jason stated, his voice a fait accompli.

William opened his eyes to see Jason lying beside him. The flesh-eating maggots had now spread to the charred flesh of his cheek. The smell was putrid and nauseating.

"The serpent did not take him, but the infernal one will."

"I don't understand," Delequa questioned. "What are you talking about? The infernal one?"

"Death comes to us all," Jason growled, "And the infernal collector always convenes. It is my job to fight him off, and to deliver those lost."

Delequa dismissed the statement. It was too much. His brain raced with ambiguity.

"Am I going crazy?" Delequa asked. The rotting specter of guilt didn't answer.

"Goddamn it," Delequa demanded, "answer me, Jason. Has this disgrace driven me mad?"

Jason extended a decrepit, skeletal hand, placing it on Delequa's shoulder. His touch was firm.

"No," Jason acknowledged, "You're not mad, battle buddy. I've not been with you to torment, but to prepare you for this day. Your visions of me are a constant reminder of the warrior that is buried deep within you, flawed and imperfect, yet ever present." Jason retracted his hand, pointing toward the sound of conflict. "Soon, you will do for another what you could not do for me."

Hearing the words, Delequa burst into tears, slamming his head into the ground, over and over. Forcefully trying to release the sorrow.

"I'm so sorry, I was young and stupid, and I failed you," he confessed, looking back to Jason. The decrepit specter was gone. The young and healthy soldier Delequa once knew peered back. Finally, the words he wanted to speak for years were spoken. Instantly, he felt as if a hundred-pound weight rose from his chest. It was a wonderful feeling. Jason smiled at his old friend.

"William, it is time. I will be with you every step of the way. Now remember who you are!"

5

The simulator did not explode. It is a dud. An experience that occurred more than munitions experts and government contractors that invented the device liked to admit. The universe must truly loathe them, but the realization did not hinder Hines' objective. The flow of adrenaline empowered him far more than anything he had ever felt before.

6

Gore dripped from Kurt's beard as he blew a sadistic kiss to his unconscious wife, the footsteps drawing ever nearer. Love was a gateway to lunacy.

7

Delequa listened, but the explosion never came. His gut began to churn at a sense of impending failure. The simulator was old. It must have malfunctioned. Fuck. The plan was FUBAR. He needed to improvise.

The air chilled around him, charged with energy, and he knew he wasn't alone. He lifted from the ground in a full sprint, zig zagging through the vegetation that stood between him and the passenger door of the vehicle. In his peripheral vision, he could see Hines closing the distance to the enemy.

"Drop the saw, motherfucker!" Hines lunged, soaring through the air like the Man of Steel himself, a final and desperate bid to disarm the nutcase.

Delequa's combat boots pushed faster and faster as the passenger door drew closer. Another lesson from his past training came to mind. Never give the reasons why you can't accomplish your task, instead give the next idea that will make it happen. A new plan had formed; assist Hines with the madman, then save the girl.

Hines disappeared behind the far side of the vehicle as Delequa slid face first into the front passenger tire. True confrontation had begun.

8

With no warning, Kurt spun, bringing the lively chainsaw to bear in an uppercut motion. The hungry teeth chewed through Hines's outstretched left arm and connected with his lower jaw. The blade burrowed through his face in an instant, exiting at his nose with a spray of blood and ground meat. The impact jolted Kurt, loosening his grip on the gore-slicked handgrip. He stumbled backwards as the heavy machinery fell to the ground, ripping up chunks of earth as the blade slowed, shutting off the small engine.

Hines landed with a thud in the summer grass. Blood gushed and spurted from his once handsome face. Bewildered, incoherent words gurgled from his gaping throat as he grabbed for the missing chin. The confusion turned to finality. A part of him belonged to the forest now. How fast the tide of battle could shift in favor of the wicked, Hines thought as his vision blurred. There was a ringing in his ears so loud it blocked all other sound. Hines knew this was why most people took no action in times of need. Not from fear of getting involved, but a fear of losing life or limb. Yet, he also knew the world needed heroes. If he could do it over again, he wouldn't hesitate. Everybody wants to be the hero until it's time to do hero shit.

9

Calhoun skidded to a stop fifteen yards from the truck and took cover behind a large tree. Kurt stood across from Hines, gritting his teeth and rubbing the pain from his hands. Calhoun analyzed the situation with pure shock. He couldn't believe their luck. The device was a dud and now Hines lay mangled and dying. Never had he been so scared.

Kurt shook the last bit of aggravation from his wrists and watched the uniformed soldier writhe in the dirt, seeking a jaw that was no longer there.

Delequa peeked under the truck and saw Hines squirming on the ground, the bottom half of his face missing. If only Calhoun could distract him, he could maneuver an attack. Violence must play out. Violence will solve everything.

"Goddamn it," Kurt complained. "Where the fuck did another soldier boy come from?"

What remained of Hines's tongue jerked from side to side among the other severed tendons and loosely hanging flesh. He was struggling to produce audible words.

"Such a sad sight to see. A deformed tragedy really! Well, that's what ya get for pokin' ya nose in other folks' bidness. Done plum lost half yer face, ain't ya?" Kurt laughed, nudging the struggling soldier. "Twisting about like that won't relieve the pain, and it damn sure won't stop the bleeding. Don't ya worry, any second now, it'll be over."

10

Hines's body stopped fighting the agony and came to rest, staring into the blue sky. The battlefield was where all soldiers intended to die, but in his final moments, the Army didn't matter, only fond memories of his wife flickered through his mind. Her lips. Her smile. Her beautiful brown hair and the sweetness in her voice.

Suddenly, Hines felt a presence. His eyes searched desperately. A fellow soldier was standing over him, someone he'd never met. The service member's face was charred. Smoke danced across his shoulders, as the sky above bled into red and pink.

"It's time to let go, brother," Jason heartened. "You're not alone. I will guide you to the light of our maker."

With a final effort of speech, Hines tried his hardest to respond. The spirit knelt, taking his hand in his final moments. Hines felt a flowing peace. One of friendship and brotherhood. He was not alone, for no soldier dies alone.

11

Calhoun knew the rescue mission was a failure, and Staff Sergeant Hines wouldn't be able to help him any longer. He was clueless as to Delequa's location. The enemy's back faced Calhoun and he wanted to attack, but a new level of fear locked the young soldier in place. All momentum was gone. The adage, "if you wish to kill a snake, you cut off the head" certainly applied in the military. Take out the leader; the others lose hope and the will to fight. Kurt had achieved that unwittingly.

Delequa placed his head against the blistering hot metal of the truck. Jason appeared before him.

"This is what makes us different, William. I'll see you again, old friend, but not today. Remember who you are. Finish the fight." Jason's words were cold and final.

12

Calhoun saw Hines stop breathing. His eyes staring to the sky, forehead furrowed, yet he looked proud. That gorgeous grin he loved to show off would never shine again. Shame blanketed Reggie Calhoun for failing to act. In full emotional breakdown, he staggered to the truck, throwing his body weight into the hood, alarming Delequa on the opposite side.

Calhoun collapsed to his knees. "Goddamn it, Sergeant," he sobbed, "please get up!"

Confounded, Kurt turned slowly to face the new adversary, taking note the chain had come loose from the chainsaw blade.

"Holy shit, we gotta 'nother one," Kurt announced.

Calhoun lifted himself up, using the vehicle as leverage. He looked down to the malfunctioned grenade simulator. He looked back to Kurt assuming a boxer's stance. Knuckles high, clenched so tight the black pigment went white, eager to brawl.

"You wanna take a shot at the title?" Kurt laughed, rolling his shoulders forward in a mock fighting stance. Kurt knew he couldn't take a trained soldier in a hand-to-hand fight, but if he could get to the gun in the truck, the black boy would join his friend. After that, he could finally finish Ava off.

Calhoun adjusted his posture, no longer scared. The young soldier's body was in autopilot. "Ring the bell, muthafucka," Calhoun snarled.

13

Delequa remained silent, shifting nervously towards the edge of the tire, tossing different scenarios around his brain. When the opportunity came, he couldn't falter. The woman remained unconscious.

"Fuck you, punk!" Kurt screamed, rushing the soldier.

Calhoun pounced towards the blood-soaked killer. Kurt sidestepped, almost making it to the door of the truck, but the feisty soldier snatched him by the flannel and delivered a massive blow to his nose, splitting it open. Kurt wobbled back, flinging a blind haymaker from his right shoulder. It connected with Calhoun's jaw but lacked conviction.

"Come on bitch," Calhoun taunted.

Kurt swung recklessly, with no precision or focus. Calhoun closed the distance, securing him by the neck with both hands, and slamming him into the side of the truck. Kurt retaliated with a swift knee to the stomach, knocking the wind out of Calhoun, followed by a brutal head-butt that struck like a lightning bolt. Calhoun's vision blurred. Kurt shoved him off, opened the truck door, and dove into the cab. Calhoun grabbed Kurt's legs, raining down heavy strikes to the man's hamstrings. Kurt howled, hands still thick with blood and too slippery to secure the weapon. Kurt kicked wildly, grazing Calhoun's face.

"Come here, motherfucker!" Calhoun screamed, pulling Kurt's legs hard. "Sergeant Delequa, help!"

Delequa had maneuvered to the rear tire. There, he came face to face with the realism of the massacre. A nightmare of death cloaked the area, true and pure. Ava twitched, beginning to wake.

Kurt shimmied far enough to finally seize the shotgun from the floorboard, a round already in the chamber. Calhoun released Kurt as he rotated to his side with the weapon in hand.

"He's got a gun," Calhoun warned. A massive boom rang out.

Buckshot destroyed the driver's side window, damaging the steering wheel and deploying the airbag. Delequa jumped from the blast.

"Come on, boy," Kurt hollered, pumping in another shell, "I got somethin' for that ass!"

With speed, Calhoun dashed from the vehicle and dove behind the tree holding Denis's remains. Swarms of flies had begun feasting on the carcass. Calhoun pressed his back against the rough bark, breathing heavily. He debated sprinting deeper into the forest, unsure if he would survive the attempt.

Kurt fought his way past the airbag. Free from the truck, his throbbing legs were unstable. The madman raised the gun.

"Bang, bang, kid!" Kurt taunted loudly, "You didn't think the belt would be that easy, did you?"

Calhoun looked to the sky and prayed.

14

Kurt continued scanning the area, admiring the blood bath. He brought his cheek to the stock. "One shot, one kill. Ain't that what you soldier boys say?" Kurt teased, "Trust me. I'll kill ya' fast."

Hyperventilating, Calhoun dug his fingers into the warm earth. Kurt heard the movement.

"You know," Kurt paused, stretching his sore neck, "I sure the fuck didn't expect things to get this excitin' today, but I got a few rounds left with your name on it." He moved toward Calhoun's location. "Bring your punk ass out, or I'll come get ya.'"

Accepting his fate, Calhoun yelled a frantic reply, tears forming, "Come and get me, asshole!"

Angered, Kurt gripped the stock tighter, the barrel targeting the edge of the tree. He tiptoed sideways, ready for the kill. Calhoun's exposed hand came into view. Kurt pulled the trigger. Calhoun screamed to the high heavens, pulling away as best he could. Examining the wound, he found small beads of steel lodged under the skin. Painful, but could have been worse. A finger could be missing.

With the roar of the gunfire, Ava opened her eyes. Kurt cocked the shotgun again, sending the spent red shell casing flying into the air. Calhoun pictured his old drill sergeant chastising him for improper cover and concealment. Kurt scrambled to the tree, the fastest he's moved all day, bringing the shotgun inches from the lamenting soldier's face.

"Fuck you, boy," Kurt spit.

"Kurt, no!" Ava screamed.

15

Kurt shifted his gaze to his beloved, locking eyes with her. Trying his darnedest to conjure another zinger, he noticed a blur from the corner of his eye. Delequa's fist landed, crushing the psycho's eye socket and sending him careening into a nearby tree. The impact was so forceful, he teetered back toward the salty soldier who wrapped his arms around the man's waist and lifted with all his might. Kurt turned ten tootsies up as Delequa leaned back into a suplex. With one last ditch effort, Kurt fumbled for control of the weapon as he careened through the air, aiming the best he could in Ava's direction, and pulled the trigger. The round soared skyward shredding leaves and a branch.

A loud crunch resounded as Kurt's neck struck the ground. Delequa rolled Kurt to his stomach, in a rear mount. There, he brought the pain. Blow after blow struck Kurt's head and face.

"Help me," Ava begged. "Please, get me down!" Her pleas went unheard. Delequa saw red as the rage enveloped him. Calhoun applied pressure to his wound and managed to get to his feet. "Sergeant, I'm coming."

In the heat of battle, Delequa dives into his pouch and pulls out the last grenade simulator.

He pops the clip and pulls the string. A loud hissing, like a lit stick of dynamite, fills the clearing. Kurt tries to buck him off, but Delequa digs his heels into the lumberjack's hips and squeezes. He lands a dazing southpaw, then a right—delivering the explosive.

The boom-boom-device comes to rest against Kurt's temple. Delequa releases it, then presses the man's head down so it stays next to the sizzling canister. Kurt's neck is fractured. It won't help him.

Calhoun stumbles from behind a tree and witnesses the end.

"Ava," Kurt squeals, eyes full of rage and sorrow.

The device detonates. Red, purple, and pink mist blooms into the wilderness. Portions of Kurt's skull fly into the air. Large shards tear into Delequa's cheeks, ripping flesh; tiny splinters pepper his face. He looks like a new kind of porcupine.

Ava watches, stunned and not fully understanding.

"Fuck me," Delequa says, bringing his hands to his face.

Calhoun rushes forward and pries Delequa off the corpse. Ava screams and collapses into tears. Calhoun hooks his arms under Delequa and drags him back toward the truck.

"You okay, Sergeant?" he asks.

"I'm fine," Delequa says, bracing himself against the truck and ignoring the bone fragments embedded in his cheeks. "Let me see your hand."

Calhoun shows him; blood and dirt coat it.

"Jesus, Sergeant," Calhoun huffs. "Your face."

"Don't worry about me," Delequa says, then inspects Calhoun's wounds. "You're gonna be fine, kid. Fight through the pain—let's get her down."

Ava's voice breaks from the tree, raw and strained. "Thank you," she sobs. "Oh my God, thank you!"

Calhoun limps toward her, avoiding Hines's lifeless body. Delequa stands and walks to Kurt. He stops inches away.

The lumberjack is dead. Fecal matter soaks through his pants—one of the first signs a body has stopped living. The stench is unbearable.

"Fuck you," Delequa says, and turns away. The fight is over.

They untie the knots binding Ava to the tree. They refuse to use the knife Kurt used to kill Denis, not wanting to contaminate evidence. Ava weeps and thanks them. Calhoun's hand throbs as he works; with a final tug the ropes come free.

Ava falls forward into Delequa's arms—battered, sunburned, broken. The soldiers avert their eyes from her injured genitals. With the little strength she has left, she wraps her arms around Delequa's neck.

In another life they could have been lovers.

"You saved me," she cries. "You didn't have to—but you saved me."

"Ma'am," Delequa says quietly, "Everything's gonna be okay. Understand?"

"You're my savior," she wails. "The Lord sent me saviors today." Delequa ignores the praise and calls to Calhoun. "Private Calhoun, help me get her into the truck."

"Roger that, Sergeant." Calhoun hesitates only to look at Hines. The loss of his leader crushes him; he collapses to his knees.

"Stay right here, okay," Delequa tells Ava. She nods.

He crouches beside Calhoun. "I failed him," the younger soldier sobs. "I stumbled, and it cost him his life."

"Listen to me, kid." Delequa shakes him until their eyes meet. "No one failed today. That man died a hero. He saved this woman."

"I don't see it that way," Calhoun says. "Nobody had to die."

"We serve a purpose, brother," Delequa says, clutching Calhoun's shoulder. "Not just in this life, but the next." He looks at Hines, at the pools of blood. "Everything happens for a reason. Don't blame yourself. You hear me?"

Calhoun nods, wiping his face. "We'll mourn, but first we get her clothed and into the truck," Delequa orders.

"Check, Sergeant." Calhoun rises.

The passenger door closes. Ava wraps Calhoun's uniform top around herself and keeps crying. The two soldiers lift Hines carefully onto the truck bed—never leave a fallen comrade. Delequa stares at the empty, honored body.

"Get in the truck, Calhoun," Delequa says. "Keep her calm while I figure out what we do next. Don't touch anything in that truck. It's all evidence."

"Roger that, Sergeant." Calhoun steps away but drags his bleeding hand across Hines's legs—a final gesture of thanks.

Delequa leans in for a quick farewell. Everyone needs medical attention, but there's one thing he hasn't done in decades. He prays.

"Father," he whispers, gripping Hines's arm and speaking so no one else hears. "Forgive me for what I've done today. Do not let this man suffer in the next life. Take his sins from him and place them on me. I beg you."

Above, the sun burns hot.

"Don't let him suffer the eternal fire. Let it be for me. This man died a hero."

A strange relief floods him—Hines's death frees something in Delequa. Guilt, regret, and grief recede. He cries hard, letting the pain out. The splinters in his face ache, but he feels forgiven. He looks around, expecting Jason to appear.

A hum vibrates in Delequa's FLC. He fumbles for his pouch and pulls out his phone.

It's working.

The device vibrates and displays the name:

JAMES

1200 HRS

1

On the far side of the clearing, one hundred yards beyond Denis's tree, a Walker with a squad of Infantry troops called out to the survivors. "This is Staff Sergeant Sorem with Task Force One, identify yourselves."

Delequa paid him no mind. The infantry squad advanced around the scene.

2

In the back of the cab, Private Calhoun shifts among the rear seats, tossing collected beer cans and Tractor Supply plastic bags to the floorboard to make room for the wounded woman.

"Would you like to lie down back here, ma'am?" Calhoun asks, kindly.

Ava doesn't answer. She only weeps from the passenger seat.

Red Rhonda, the gas-guzzling Nissan Titan, blows cold air into the cab and brings much-needed relief.

"Want more air on you, ma'am?"

"It's Ava," she says, voice weak and hollow. "My name is Ava."

"Okay," Calhoun says calmly. "Ava, would you like me to turn the vent?"

"Yes." Ava drifts back into sorrow. "Why'd he do this to me?" she whispers. "He was my husband."

Calhoun can't answer that. It's a question that may never be answered. Seconds later the waterworks begin again. Calhoun rubs her shoulder gently. He leans forward to adjust the vent on the right side and looks out the front window. He notices the Walker and a squad of soldiers approaching from the brush. For the first time in hours he feels something besides fear. Excitement overtakes him.

"Look, ma'am," Calhoun says, pointing, "they've found us!"

Ava says nothing. She just sits and cries.

Calhoun looks out the window again and, for a moment, sees Staff Sergeant Hines. The apparition stands in the distance where they'd started the assault on the lumberjack. His face is handsome again, full of confidence and spunk. He looks at Calhoun and gives a small wave.

"What the—" Calhoun mutters.

"Kurt," Ava whispers.

Calhoun breaks the vision and glances at the woman. "Why'd you do this to me," she asks again, shoulders shaking.

He refocuses on the spot where Shelton Hines had stood moments before; beyond the windshield there is only oppressive heat and uncultivated wilderness.

In the darkest hour
When the demons come
Call on me, brother
And we will fight them together

J.P. Willie is a Louisiana-born horror author and filmmaker, and a retired U.S. Army soldier. He graduated from Tara High School in Baton Rouge, Louisiana, and enlisted in the United States Army on October 20, 2000.

During his military career, he was stationed at Fort Bragg (North Carolina), Caserma Ederle (Italy), Mannheim (Germany), Fort Benning (Georgia), Schofield Barracks (Hawaii), Fort Polk (Louisiana), and Joint Base Elmendorf-Richardson (Alaska). He completed two combat tours in Afghanistan with the 82nd Airborne Division and the 173rd Airborne Brigade, retiring honorably after twenty-one years of service in 2021.

Willie began his writing career in March 2008. His debut novel, *Blood in the Woods*, published by HellBound Books Publishing on December 18, 2017, was inspired by true events from his childhood and has terrified readers worldwide. His short story, "Welcome Home Rougarou," reached #5 in Amazon's Short Reads category.

His directorial debut, *Crybaby Bridge: A Louisiana Urban Legend*, won Best Short Film at the Horror in the Heat Film Festival and placed third at the Lake Charles Film Festival. Produced on a zero budget with first-time cast and crew, the film was later selected for The Louisiana Film Channel, a streaming service dedicated to Louisiana-based film and television.

For his second film, *Welcome Home Rougarou*, Willie served as writer, director, and editor. Shot along the Blind River in Lake Maurepas, Louisiana, the film is available to watch on YouTube.

J.P. Willie writes horror, psychological thrillers, supernatural fiction, and dark fiction. His first novella, *Hot Summer Savior*, was published by Nightmare Press in 2026.

ALSO AVAILABLE FROM NIGHTMARE PRESS

THE GUARDIANS

Teresa Sewell & Rob Le

In a mystical world where lycans and vampires rule, where magic, cruelty, and blood are part of everyday life, in a time if good fails then all is lost, fate rests in the hands of three people. Three spoken of in a forgotten legend from a race destroyed long ago—or a perhaps a race long hidden from those who seek to destroy them.

Brenat and Teera believe they'll never conceive. However, a miracle happens during their bonding on the night of the blood moon, bringing the couple both surprise and joy. When a second miracle occurs, and they find themselves with seven children, they dream of raising their family in the safety of a small, hidden valley.

Threatening their dream are those who want the children for their own evil schemes. The eldritch witch Keres and her wicked master seek to annihilate all that is good in the world. Believing the family to be those spoken of in the ancient legend of creation, Keres and her master set out to gain control of the children and convert them to evil so they can rule the world.

However, they are not the only ones with nefarious plans for Joel and his siblings...

FAM

John Shupeck

Seventeen-year-old Trevor Taylor has lived his short life being ruled by addiction. Not wanting to be alone in his misery, he takes his little brother, eleven-year-old Dustin, along for the ride, until one fateful night when a freak drug lab explosion kills the elder brother, along with his two partners.

"God, please let him come back," Dustin prays every night, begging whatever watches above to let him see his brother one last time.

Unfortunately, what watches above is always listening, and it is not God.

Dustin, now seventeen himself, begins to have a creeping suspicion that he and his mother, Desta, are not alone in the house anymore, and that Trevor may have returned to have one last adventure.

Lies, gaslighting, and past abuses soon come to light, showing that sometimes the true horror comes not from what we can't see, but from what stands right in front of us, silently feeding off of our sanity until we are consumed.

WHITE TRASH SUBLIME

Dickson Lee Turpin

Eldritch horrors beset Meridian's white trash, who must survive the sublime. A mere utterance from beyond unravels reality and infects the flesh, turning them into shrieking travesties. Told through mad tales, they explore terror and the failings of the human heart.

OCCULTATION

Eric Lahti

On a long-abandoned alien space station orbiting a mysterious black object, the rules are different. Whether it's the immersive virtual reality that's indistinguishable from reality, the wild bazaar where anything and everything is for sale, the drunken debauchery, or the group of giants who run everything and keep the peace, Endpoint is the place where people go to do what they'd never do anywhere else.

For instance, two nights ago, a hacker deleted her brain. This morning a thief awoke in her body with a task: *Find out what happened and you'll get your body back.*

Now, Nat will have to navigate the madness, cults, and twisted power structures to find answers. But on Endpoint, nothing is ever simple.

And the abandoned alien space station may not be as abandoned as everyone thought.

KENTUCKY'S HAUNTED GRAVEYARDS

The Frightening Floyds

From The Frightening Floyds—authors of *Kentucky's Strange and Unusual Haunts*, *Aliens Over Kentucky*, and many other books on the mysterious and paranormal—comes *Kentucky's Haunted Graveyards*, a collection of spooky stories from various cemeteries across the Bluegrass State.

Within this book you will find abandoned cemeteries filled with spirits, celebrities' graves, a glowing tombstone, a haunted mausoleum, a sprawling necropolis filled with exquisite monuments, a woman in search of her black cat, a graveyard said to hold the Gates of Hell, and many more.

There are also some cemeteries not exactly haunted, but very strange and very unusual. Among them are a pet cemetery with a dark history, a haunting procession of lifelike statues, the bones of centuries-old martyrs displayed in a church, human bodies interred at a zoo, a family plot in a parking lot, and an airport and business compound built around a Native burial ground.

Join Jacob and Jenny Floyd as they bring you these creepy and weird stories in *Kentucky's Haunted Graveyards.*

ALADDIN'S CURSE

Mark Pickvet

A magic lamp containing an evil Djinni embarks upon an incredible journey as it passes from the Stone Age to the Modern World. The malevolent Djinni fulfills the wishes of those who gain possession of his lamp, only those wishes do not always come out exactly as planned. Tragedy fills *Aladdin's Curse,* as little to no good comes to those who wish for personal gain from the ancient magic. Only three unselfish wishes can rid the world of this wicked force. Follow the series of subplots and short stories through time as the lamp and the evil spirit within all uniquely interconnect them.

The dark side of human nature is only a wish away. As the old saying goes: "Be careful what you wish for; you just might get it!"

BREAKING THE DEVIL'S BREAD: DARK WORDS AND SHADOW TALES

Satyros Phil Brucato

Our lives are made of stories.

Some of those tales get pretty damn dark.

In the following "13 stories and an Oops," award-winning dark fantasist Satyros Phil Brucato (*Red Shoes*, *Mage*, *Valhalla with a Twist of Lethe*) explores shadows, cries, and silence.

Careless haunters, elite collectors, secretive enforcers, lip-synching goths, hapless custodians, strange children, subterranean exiles, tortured fiends, harried jesters, haggard coulrophobes, ragged batterers, joyous hikers, carnal mystics, and exploding cosmos tell their tales as sardonic darkness swallows all.

If mortal dread is the Devil's bread, then we're all welcome at the feast.

THE HURDY GURDY MAN

David Turnbull

Set in London in the summer of 1969, *The Hurdy Gurdy Man* follows Kath Dunn, who has left her home near the seaside town Berwick on Tweed, and finds herself homeless on the streets of Piccadilly. Here she encounters the eccentric Gordon Urquhart-Scott, who persuades Kath to accompany him to his large crumbling home on the edge of Hampstead Heath, where he claims to run a hostel for homeless women.

Kath finds herself inducted as one of twelve formerly homeless women who reside free of charge in the house in exchange for obeying the Hurdy Gurdy Man's strange rules, including nightly musical performances on the hand-cranked hurdy-gurdy from which his nickname derives.

Kath befriends Ruth. Together they secretly unravel terrible truths linked to the British Class system, the establishment, and the gruesome Scottish borders legends of the Redcaps. After witnessing how deep the horror within the decaying home truly runs, the two women decide to confront the evil at its source. Enlisting the help of other women, they engineer a terrifying conflict they hope will send the evil back to whatever foul region of darkness from whence it came.

BELINDA'S KEYBOARDS
PART ONE: DED'S LINE

Dedham Pond

Dedham Pond is a journalist in his fifties rediscovering how to do his job responsibly in an era that appreciates bias over truth and influencers over experts. While investigating the death of an old friend's son, Ded discovers Belinda Blessing, who is part of a conspiracy of people who enjoy injecting discord and chaos into the culture wherever they can. Now Ded must find a way to stop the destruction caused by Belinda's keyboards and bring her to justice.

SARAH CORBIN'S BLOODY REVENGE

Coyote Wallace

When Sarah Corbin and her family are killed in a midnight robbery gone wrong, she makes a deal for her mortal soul - in exchange for the chance to hunt down the men who burned her world to ash.

Violent, unflinching, and tinged with supernatural overtones, *Sarah Corbin's Bloody Revenge* takes readers into the dark heart of Texas, where the air is heavy with gun smoke and the streets run red.

On the other end of Sarah's revenge is Lono Talbot, a murderous cutthroat who has parlayed stolen gold into a position of power in the small town of Gehenna. His network of gunslingers and outlaws, reinforced with his ill-gotten gains, has made him one of the most powerful men in the Texas underground. Too well protected for lawmen, Lono continues to grow his influence and power....

....until the mistakes of his past come calling.

READ MORE NIGHTMARE PRESS!!!

Visit our website at nightmarepress5.wordpress.com

Also, follow us on:

Facebook: https://www.facebook.com/nightmarepress1

Instagram: https://www.instagram.com/nightmarepress1

Join the Nightmare Press Group on Facebook to interact with our authors, and keep abreast of their creative endeavors.

www.ingramcontent.com/pod-product-compliance
Lightning Source LLC
LaVergne TN
LVHW091143080826
845145LV00008B/2241
* 9 7 8 1 6 4 9 0 5 0 4 3 4 *